The Three Boys

The Three Boys

And Other Buddhist Folktales
from Tibet

Told and Illustrated by
Yeshi Dorjee

Transcribed and Edited by
John S. Major

A Latitude 20 Book
University of Hawai'i Press
Honolulu

Library of Congress Cataloging-in-Publication Data

The three boys and other Buddhist folk tales from Tibet /
told and illustrated by Yeshi Dorjee ; transcribed and
edited by John S. Major.

    p. cm.

Some tales adapted from Vetalapañcavimsati.
Includes bibliographical references.
ISBN-13: 978-0-8248-3079-3 (pbk. : alk. paper)
ISBN-10: 0-8248-3079-2 (pbk. : alk. paper)
1. Tales—China—Tibet. I. Dorjee, Yeshi, 1960– .
II. Major, John S. III. Vetalapañcavimsati. IV. Title.
GR337.T45 2007
398.20951'5—dc22

                        2006006229

Designed by University of Hawai'i Press production staff
Printed by Versa Printers

Contents

Introduction

Today, Yeshi Dorjee radiates the confident serenity that seems to be a hallmark of Buddhist monks, but his life got off to a tumultuous and difficult start. He was conceived in Tibet but born in Bhutan, a small, isolated country in the Himalayan mountains between Tibet and the northeastern border of India, where his parents had fled in 1960 to escape the consequences of the Chinese invasion of Tibet the year before. The Dalai Lama had already made his way to India, and hundreds of thousands of Tibetans followed him into exile. But for Yeshi's family, the safety of Bhutan soon turned into a nightmare. His father died there when Yeshi was only seven months old; he has no memory of him. Then, before he was two years old, his sister, grandmother, and uncle also died, leaving Yeshi and his mother to face the world alone. "I think things were difficult for my mother," Yeshi recalls with a shy smile.

After several years of trying to remain single and support Yeshi and herself as a widow, Yeshi's mother yielded to pressure from her relatives and remarried. She had other children with her new husband, and her new family gave her much more security than she had before. But it was a mixed blessing. Her new mother-in-law was very hostile to her and made her life difficult both physically and emotionally. Sometimes her husband sided with his mother and treated his new wife harshly. All of this affected Yeshi, too; he was always acutely aware that he was the son of a different father, and he never felt that he truly belonged in his new family. His childhood was secure, but it was not necessarily happy.

Yeshi's childhood interests show a desire to escape from the harsh realities of his life. From an early age, he loved to draw and paint, and drawing pictures was a means of creating for himself a life of beauty and fantasy based on the traditional imagery of Tibetan Buddhist art. He also loved stories and persuaded older people to tell him the traditional folktales of Tibet whenever he could. And from the age of seven, he began to think that he wanted to become a Buddhist monk.

He kept this ambition to himself for a couple of years. Then one day a man came to his school—a visitor from India who described life in the Tibetan exile community there and the new institutions of Tibetan higher learning that were being established to serve the religious needs of that community. Yeshi immediately felt that it was his great chance to make his way to India to study to become a monk. But how would he manage it? Who would help him? So he was extremely surprised when he went home from school to find the visitor chatting with his mother; he was even more surprised to learn that the man was his uncle, an uncle he had never heard of. Soon Yeshi confided to him his ambition to become a monk.

Yeshi's uncle questioned him closely about his decision to see if he was truly serious. When he was fully convinced, he told Yeshi that he would sponsor him to study in India if he could get his mother's permission. Yeshi's mother tried to discourage him by pointing out all of the difficulties he would face. For starters, how would he get to India? Wouldn't he be lonely there, so far from his mother? But Yeshi did not give up. "After I asked her many times, I wore down her resistance," Yeshi says, laughing. "So she finally said okay." Soon after, he began his studies at Gyudmed Tantric University in Karnataka, India. He would be a student there for the next twenty-five years.

It was in his early years at the university, before he turned fourteen, that Yeshi learned most of the traditional folktales he can recite today. Some he learned from his uncles in early childhood, but most he heard from the older monks at the university. He learned to make himself useful to these older monks, in exchange for them telling him stories. For example, usually the monks lived four to a room, and at mealtimes the youngest monk was expected to go to the kitchen to bring back food for all of them. Sometimes Yeshi would volunteer to fetch meals for older monks who lived in rooms without a young student; by winning their goodwill, he was able to coax them into teaching him stories in their spare time. At planting time in the spring, Yeshi liked to work in the fields with the elderly monks. When planting corn, an old monk would walk ahead, dropping the seed in the furrow, while Yeshi would walk behind him, covering up the seeds with soil and listening as the monk told a story to pass the time.

In his many years at Gyudmed University, Yeshi absorbed a comprehensive curriculum of Tantric Buddhist studies, leading to the degree of *Geshe Ngarampa* (the Buddhist equivalent of a PhD). His special field was Buddhist devotional arts; he became a specialist in the painting of devotional images *(thangka)* as well as the related arts of butter sculpture and sand mandalas. He also became an expert and prize-winning practitioner of the art of Tibetan calligraphy. But always in addition to his formal studies, Yeshi learned traditional Tibetan Buddhist stories whenever the opportunity arose—not as an academic discipline, but as both an avocation that enriched his own life and a personal contribution to the great project of the Tibetan community in exile to preserve as much as possible of the old culture and knowledge of Tibet.

Yeshi plans to remain in the United States for the indefinite future. His goal in this country is to establish a School of Tibetan Sacred Arts where American and international students of Buddhism can learn the motifs and techniques of *thangka* painting and related Tibetan arts. Yeshi's royalties from the sale of this book will be devoted to that project.

DURING THE twentieth century, anthropologists and folklore scholars collected hundreds of folktales in Tibet and other parts of Inner Asia, recording the words of storytellers in towns and villages, caravan camps and oasis inns, monasteries and taverns—wherever people gathered to share a good story. Many of these tales exist in dozens of variations found over a huge geographical area: Tibet, Turkistan, China, Mongolia, and beyond. Some of them originated in Buddhist culture but are now found in other cultures as well (e.g., in Islamic and Daoist cultures); some originated elsewhere and were assimilated into Buddhism. One tale, for example, generically known as "The Tale of the Ugly Girl" (and included in this collection as "King Salgyel's Daughter, Princess Dorjee") exists in versions in Tibetan, Chinese, Uighur, Kyrgiz, Kazak, Mongolian, and several other Inner Asian languages. Like many of these tales, it is also very old: one version is found on a scroll that was written about a thousand years ago and preserved in the Buddhist library at Dunhuang. Remarkably, even certain phrases in these many versions of the story crop up over and over again (e.g., the ugly princess is typically described as having hair like coconut fiber and skin like the bark of a tree).

Written versions of several of the other tales in this book can be found in the *Vetâlapañcaviṃśati* (Twenty-five corpse tales), a collection of stories thought to have been compiled in the eleventh century, drawing upon earlier sources. The original collection is in

Sanskrit; the work has been translated into Tibetan and many other languages. Thus, there are published versions of many of the stories that Yeshi learned orally. The stories in different editions of the *Vetâlapañcaviṃśati* are recognizably the same, but they often vary widely in specific details. Similarly, the stories as Yeshi learned them differ in many details from the published versions. Stories evolve as they are written, revised, and edited, or told and retold; in other words, stories belong to lineages that diverge over time.

Of the hundreds of extant Tibetan folktales, Yeshi Dorjee learned several dozen in the course of his childhood, not just in the sense of having heard them once or twice, but in the deeper sense of having absorbed them thoroughly so that he can retell them nearly word-for-word as he learned them from his teachers. Of those dozens, we present a selection of fifteen in this collection. It is our hope and intention that they will convey something of the richness, the wisdom, and the delight of this amazing tradition of oral literature.

This book is not intended to be a scholarly study of Tibetan folklore and folk literature. There is already a large body of scholarship in those fields, tracing, for example, the variant versions of Tibetan folktales and comparing them with versions of the same or similar tales in other cultures. Some of the most salient works in the field of Tibetan folk literature are listed in the "Suggestions for Further Reading" at the end of this book. Our goal in writing this book has been to present to readers particular oral versions of these stories as they were learned by one young monk at the feet of his elders. If scholars will take these versions into consideration in their comparative studies, Yeshi and I will be very pleased. If students of Tibetology, Buddhology, and folklore will find them of interest, we will be pleased by that as well. But we will be happiest of all if these stories are read by a large number of laypeople

who are interested in Tibet, in Buddhism, or in folk literature, or
who just know how to enjoy a good story.

One might wonder why Buddhism is so rich in folk literature in the first place. The answer lies in the special feature of Buddhism, which like Christianity and Islam (and in sharp contrast to
many other religions, such as Hinduism and Shinto) is a strongly
proselytizing faith. That is, many Buddhist believers—and especially Buddhist lamas and monks—feel a strong obligation to
acquaint other people, who perhaps have not heard or absorbed
the good news of Buddhism, with the truth of the Buddhist sal-
vationist message. (Buddhists are, however, careful not to impose
their beliefs on others; they only proselytize to people who express
an interest in hearing their message.) A strong tradition grew in
Buddhism whereby wandering lamas and monks would teach in
town squares and marketplaces to whomever wanted to listen. And
what better way to illustrate some of the points of their teaching
than with a good story?

That circumstance accounts in turn for the character of the
stories themselves, which are often earthy, funny, full of complicated twists and turns, and seemingly lacking in any overt religious message. They have none of the Sunday-school quality of
treacly piety that makes many didactically religious stories seem
insipid and uninteresting. (The story of "The Shape-Shifter's Son,"
though full of monsters and even cannibalism, is unusual among
the stories in this collection because of its explicitly didactic focus
on a religious dharma teaching: all acts have consequences.) These
stories were intended to illustrate specific points of Buddhist doctrine. A Buddhist monk presenting a teaching to a willing crowd
in a marketplace might tell (or perhaps chant, accompanying himself on a stringed instrument) one of these stories both to hold the
crowd's interest and illustrate his doctrinal message. For example,
a teaching about the long reach of karma across many lifetimes

might prompt the monk to tell the story of Princess Dorjee; after he reached the rousing conclusion of the story he might ask, "And why do you think Princess Dorjee changed from an ugly woman to a beautiful one when she prayed to the Buddha?" And so the teaching would continue.

In this collection, we discuss the deeper meaning of the stories in a separate section ("Notes on the Stories") at the end of the book. Like the wandering monks of old, we want the messages conveyed by these stories to be available to our readers but not intrude on their enjoyment of the stories themselves. But a few general comments about the stories are in order here. First, the reader will notice that they vary considerably in length. A few of them are not even a thousand words long and seem at first glance almost more like extended "shaggy dog story" jokes than folktales with a religious subtext (e.g., "The Woodcutter and His Son"). Others extend to nearly ten thousand words and take a considerable time to tell aloud. Obviously these stories served different purposes for different audiences. All are part of the Buddhist preacher's repertory, but some are equally suitable for entertaining a crowd of friends over drinks in a tavern, for helping to pass the time when working at a tiresome task, or for making the miles seem shorter while trudging along on an extended journey.

That leads to a second noteworthy point, which is that seven of the fifteen stories in this collection adopt exactly the trope of tales told to pass the time on a long journey. The journey is a specific one and used as a recurring framing device for these tales. It is the story of the Buddhist ascetic saint Lord Nagarjuna, his young disciple Dersang, and the corpse-monster (a sort of re-animated corpse, or zombie) Ngudup Dorjee, whom Dersang is supposed to capture and bring back to Nagarjuna's cave. Dersang can only succeed in his task if he is able to make the journey without saying anything at all, a restriction that gives him great difficulty.

Plucky but easily distracted, Dersang tries and fails again and again. Each time, after he has been captured and is being carried in a sack back to the cave, the wily Ngudup Dorjee tells Dersang a wonderful story to tempt him to speak, with unfortunate consequences. The Ngudup Dorjee stories are an important and well-known component of the Tibetan folklore tradition. Yeshi Dorjee can recite sixteen of them (the Sanskrit compilation *Vetâlapañca-vimśati,* as its title indicates, contains a total of twenty-five such corpse tales); we include seven of them here not only because they are wonderful stories but because of how they give continuity and structure to the collection overall. In an attempt to emulate how monks or other wandering storytellers might choose to tell one story or another depending on circumstances, we have not grouped all of the Ngudup Dorjee stories together; rather, we have interspersed them among other stories.

A third point to reiterate and emphasize is that many of these stories are quite earthy and direct. They depict a world of human frailty rather than one of idealized piety. In a world of perfect Buddhist compassion, naughty boys would not throw stones at a crow's nest, but they do here, setting in train some remarkable consequences. In one or another of these tales a simple-minded boy unintentionally beats his father on the head with a rock; a good-natured charlatan concocts some strange mumbo-jumbo to impress a crowd; a precious piece of turquoise is lost in a clump of cow dung; a cook serves cat stew to a king. We can imagine a marketplace crowd hundreds of years ago roaring with laughter as the wandering monk or professional bard tells of these and other strange occurrences, rolling his eyes, making broad gestures with his hands, modulating his voice to entertain the crowd. These stories have lived by being heard and retold for centuries; we hope that they live still in these pages.

A final noteworthy point is how conspicuously these stories

belong to an oral tradition. There is a conscious use in many of them of formulaic phrases and stock settings, such as a storyteller or bard would have as part of his standard repertoire of devices. A few of the stories in this collection, notably "The King's Heart" and "The Dream Eater," display a very well-known feature of oral literature, which is that a subordinate character will explain in detail to one of the protagonists something that is going to happen; it then takes place as foretold, repeated in the story in almost exactly the same words. (This is reminiscent of the proverbial advice about how to give a good sermon: "Tell them what you're going to tell them; then tell them; then tell them what you told them.") An astute and knowing audience for oral tales expects such devices and revels in them.

Our method for recording these stories in writing was simple, and it is congruent, we hope, with the oral tradition from which the stories descend. On a series of visits to the Land of Compassion Buddha Center, near Los Angeles, where Yeshi has been living as a guest teacher and artist-in-residence for several years, I spent a couple of hours each morning with him as he told me a story or two. I taped each story for reference, but my main effort was put into mindful listening, trying to keep the story and all of its details in my own head. In the afternoon I would return to my hotel and type out the story on my laptop, referring to the tape when necessary. My aim was to convey the story in smooth, idiomatic English while remaining absolutely faithful to the details of the narrative and trying to convey as much as possible the specific phrasing and pacing of Yeshi's oral delivery. In the evening I would print out the results of the day's work at a local copy shop and deliver the manuscript to Yeshi at the start of our next day's session for him to read and correct. When I was back in New York between our storytelling sessions, Yeshi worked on the lovely illustrations that give this book an extra dimension of Tibetan flavor.

One specific point about the telling of the stories should be noted here. Traditionally, storytellers have often told these tales without giving names to many, or even any, of the main characters: they were simply "the king," "the orphan," "the prince," and so on. We, on the other hand, have usually supplied names for the main characters where tradition has not already supplied them, because in a collection of stories, the repetition of nameless kings, princesses, and orphans from story to story tends to become confusing and lacking in individuation. The characters in these stories are not just generic figures, but protagonists in separate tales, and we wanted to make that clear by giving them names: Prince Rinchen, Princess Lhamo, and so on. Yeshi emphasizes that this is very much a part of the oral tradition: "It is the storyteller's right to give the characters any names he wants."

YESHI DORJEE has been an ideal collaborator on a project that has been a pure pleasure from start to finish; he has my warmest thanks. A number of family members and close friends were among the early readers of these stories, and many of them pointed out to me the very pleasant fact that they can be enjoyed equally by grownups, young adults, and children. I would like to give special thanks to my wife, Valerie Steele, and our son, Steve; Wendy Fairey, her daughter, Emily, and her grandson, Sam; Elizabeth Choi; Tamsen Schwartzman; and Deborah Kaple and her children, Alex and Maya.

Yeshi thanks his uncle, Jamyang Choedak, and his teacher, Lobsang Kalden, who first told him these stories many years ago and whose memory he honors by passing the stories along in this book to be enjoyed and learned by others. He also thanks his niece, Chimi Paldon, for teaching him English and thus enabling him to communicate these stories to the wider world.

Both Yeshi and I thank the two anonymous expert readers who vetted the manuscript of this book for the University of Hawai'i Press and whose helpful remarks were especially important in ensuring that the "Notes on the Stories" were as accurate and useful as possible. We are also grateful for the expertise and enthusiasm of our editor at the press, Masako Ikeda.

John S. Major
New York and Los Angeles, 2005

The Three Boys

Once upon a time, in a certain kingdom, there were three boys who were very close friends. The first, Jigme, was a prince, a son of the king who lived in a grand palace. The second, Wang-chuk, was the son of a rich family; he lived in a big, beautiful house near the center of the city. The third boy, whose name was Der-sang, was an orphan. He was very poor and lived alone in a hut. But in spite of how different their backgrounds were, the boys were the best of friends; they were together every day and always found new ways to have adventures.

One day, Prince Jigme said to his friends, "I'm feeling a bit depressed today. I don't want to play in the palace or go anywhere in the city. Maybe it would help me to cheer up if we went and played in the forest." Of course, his friends agreed that if that was what he wanted, that's what they would do. So they walked out through the city gates and entered the deep, dark forest that lay beyond the city's edge.

After they had walked for some distance into the forest, they saw a big rock, rising up almost like a cliff. Growing out of the rock was a single tall tree. And in the tree was a crow's nest.

"Let's get some stones and see if we can knock down that nest," said Prince Jigme. So they walked around looking for stones until they had filled the folds of their robes with them, and then came back and put them in a pile near the base of the tree.

"Wait a minute," said the prince. "Before we start, let's show that we are serious about what we are doing. Let's swear an oath together. I'll start: I swear that I will not leave this forest, no matter what, until I have knocked down that crow's nest."

"Good idea," said Wangchuk. "I swear, too: I will not leave this forest, no matter what, until I have knocked down that crow's nest."

"I also swear that I will not leave this forest, no matter what, until I have knocked down that crow's nest," said Dersang, the orphan boy.

Then they began to throw stones at the nest. They threw many stones and hit the nest with some of them, but the nest did not move. After several hours, there were stones scattered all around the base of the tree and a few sticks had come loose from the nest, but otherwise the nest was fine.

"Oh, forget it," said Prince Jigme. "I'm going home."

"What about your oath?" said Wangchuk.

"I don't care about that," said Jigme. "It was a stupid oath in the first place because it was about something that had no meaning and no importance. Who cares if we knock down the crow's nest or not? I'm a prince, and my father is the most powerful man in the kingdom. Who will dare to criticize me if I break my oath?" And saying that, he walked away. "Let's do something else tomorrow."

"Well," said Wangchuk after Prince Jigme had left, "he might not care about keeping his word, but I care about mine. I'm going to knock down this nest or never leave the forest."

But after a couple more hours of throwing stones, the nest was as strongly lodged in the treetop as ever, and the sun was beginning to sink toward the horizon. The boys' arms were tired, and they were not having fun at all anymore.

"That's it," said Wangchuk. "I'm leaving."

"What about your oath?" asked Dersang.

"I've tried hard to keep my word, but I don't see why I should stay in this forest forever just because that stupid nest won't fall out of its tree. My father is very rich, and my house is full of servants. They will worry about me if I don't get home soon, but they certainly won't blame me for breaking my word about something as meaningless as this oath. Why don't you come with me?"

"I understand why you want to go home," said Dersang. "But I can't. Jigme's family is powerful, and that gives him enough pride to disregard a meaningless oath like this. Your family is very rich; you have enough pride in your wealth to not have to worry if you break your word in some small matter. But I am poor. I don't own anything at all. What do I have to hold on to except for my word? You go home now. I'm going to knock this nest down no matter what, and if I succeed, I'll see you tomorrow."

The rich boy went home, and Dersang continued to throw stones at the nest for several more hours, even after the sun had set and the forest was becoming very dark. No matter what he did, the nest would not budge from the tree.

Dersang sat down to think about what he should do, when suddenly an old man with a long white beard came out of a small cave in the face of the big rock. The entrance to the cave was so small that the boys had not noticed it at all before then. Moving much more quickly than you would expect an old man to be able to do, the hermit scrambled down the face of the rock. Before the orphan boy had time to think, the old man grabbed him by the neck and slammed him hard against the ground—once, twice, three times—until the wind was knocked out of his body and he almost fainted.

"What is the meaning of all this?" shouted the old man. "Why do I have to put up with nasty, ill-behaved boys throwing stones at my cave all day, and even after dark? Don't think I don't know who you are. You are the orphan boy named Dersang, and you are really in trouble now."

"I'm very sorry, sir," said Dersang, "but we didn't even know you were there. You see, we took an oath to throw stones at that crow's nest until we knocked it down, and . . ."

"Yes, yes, I heard all that nonsense," said the old man. "Well, you'd better stop now. I am Nagarjuna, and I have been meditating in that cave for years. I am very annoyed with you for disturbing me. On the other hand, now that you're here, maybe you can do something for me. It involves going on a long journey—longer than my old legs will carry me anymore—and if you succeed, you will help me bring blessings to thousands of suffering beings."

"Lord Nagarjuna, I would be honored to help you if I could. What do I need to do?" asked Dersang.

"You must first of all travel through this forest for many days until you come out the other side," said Nagarjuna. "Then you will see a hillside covered with a huge cemetery. That cemetery is full of ghosts and spirits, and your task will be to capture one of them. Not just any one, but a particular corpse-monster called Ngudup Dorjee. I have learned a magic spell that applies to that one undead corpse in particular. If you can capture him and bring him here, I will recite the spell and turn him into a big lump of gold. It will be enough gold to buy food for many thousands of poor people; that is why I say this will be a great blessing. Are you willing to do all this?"

"I certainly will try," said Dersang.

"Good," replied Nagarjuna. "Now I will give you what you need for your task. The first is a container of food. It looks very small, but this is a special kind of food; you only need to eat a little bit at a time, and you will have all the strength and nourishment you need to accomplish your task. The second thing is an axe, and the third is a big sack with a leather strap. In a minute I will tell you what those things are for.

"Now when you get to the cemetery, the first thing you must do is find a way in. You might try first from the west; if that doesn't work, try from the east. If that doesn't work, try from the south, then from the north. I don't know which way will bring you success, but you must get inside the cemetery gates.

"Once you are inside, you must call out, 'Where is Ngudup Dorjee?' Then hundreds of spirits will crowd around you, all of them saying, 'I am Ngudup Dorjee, I am Ngudup Dorjee.' But the real Ngudup Dorjee will not be among them; they are just trying to confuse you. Instead, you must look carefully for one spirit that is trying to get away from you, for that will be the real Ngudup Dorjee. If you run after him, you will see him climb up to the top of a tall tree, just like this tree with the crow's nest that you were throwing stones at.

"When you have chased him up his tree, you must say to him, 'Ngudup Dorjee, will you come down from your tree?' Of course, he will refuse. Then say, 'Ngudup Dorjee, if you don't climb down, I will chop down your tree and make you fall.' He will not be able to stand the thought of your chopping down his tree, so when you take out your axe and get ready to go to work, he will rush down the tree and try to escape. That is when you must seize him by the neck and stuff him into the sack, which you will tie closed with the leather strap.

"Now listen carefully, for this is the hardest part. Once Ngudup Dorjee is stuffed into the sack and the sack is tied closed with the leather strap, he will not be able to escape *as long as you do not say a single word to him.* He is very clever, and he will try to trick you. Keep your mouth closed no matter what. If you say even one word, the spell that keeps the sack closed will be broken, and he will fly out of it before you can stop him, and all of your hard work will have been for nothing. Not one word, do you understand? Do you think you can do that?"

"I understand, Lord Nagarjuna," said Dersang. "I promise I will not say even a single word to him, no matter what tricks he plays on me."

EVERYTHING HAPPENED in exactly the way Lord Nagarjuna predicted. Dersang journeyed for several days through the forest and when he emerged on the other side, he saw a big cemetery full of spirits. After several tries, he was able to find his way inside. He called out, "Where is Ngudup Dorjee?" and hundreds of spirits answered, "Here I am. Here. I am Ngudup Dorjee. Look over here." But one spirit, a corpse-monster, tried to get away without saying anything, and Dersang followed him and chased him up a tree.

"Ngudup Dorjee, will you come down from your tree?" cried Dersang.

"I will not," answered the spirit.

Dersang replied, "Ngudup Dorjee, if you don't climb down, I will chop down your tree and make you fall."

"Don't do that," the spirit called down to Dersang. "There's no need for you to do that." And suddenly he rushed down the tree and tried to dodge past the boy.

But the boy was too fast for him. He grabbed Ngudup Dorjee by the neck, stuffed him into the sack, and tied the sack closed with the leather strap. Slinging the bundle over his shoulders, he started walking toward the forest again to bring his prize back to Lord Nagarjuna so he could turn him into a big lump of gold.

"Say, boy, what's your name?" said Ngudup Dorjee from inside the sack.

Dersang just kept walking with his lips firmly pressed closed.

"It's going to be a long walk back to the cave, boy," said Ngudup Dorjee. "Don't you think it would be good to pass the time somehow? You could tell me a story."

Dersang walked grimly onward and said nothing.

"Not very friendly, are you, boy?" said the spirit. "How about if I tell you a story instead?"

Of course, Dersang did not reply to that either.

"I'll take that answer to mean yes," said Ngudup Dorjee. "So, since you asked, I'll entertain us both with a story. Here it goes."

ONCE UPON a time, in a certain kingdom, there were three boys who were very close friends. The first, whose name was Jigme, was a prince, a son of the king, who lived in a grand palace. The second, named Wangchuk, was the son of a rich family; he lived in a big, beautiful house near the center of the city. The third boy was an orphan, who was very poor and lived alone in a hut. His name was Dersang. In spite of how different their backgrounds were, the boys were the best of friends; they were together every day and always found new ways to have adventures.

("How strange," thought Dersang. "These three boys sound just like my friends and me.")

It so happened that in that same city there was an extremely beautiful girl who lived alone in a house with just her female servants. She was so beautiful that all of the men in town were in love with her, but she had no interest in men whatsoever. She would not even appear in the same room with anyone who was male, much less speak to a boy or man, and so all of the people who were in love with her despaired of ever winning her hand.

One day, the three friends were talking about this mysterious girl, and Prince Jigme suggested that they, too, should try to persuade her to marry one of them.

"But why should she pay attention to us?" asked Wangchuk. "After all, it is obvious that she hates men, so of course she will hate us, too. I don't think we have a chance."

"Nonsense," said the prince. "Aren't we superior to all of the other men in town? Once we succeed in speaking with her, she surely will choose one of the three of us to be her husband. But we can make the game even more interesting. Let's make a bet about which one of us will win her hand. How about this: If I succeed in winning the hand of this beautiful girl, you, my rich friend, will give me half of everything you own. Dersang does not own anything, so if I win he will have to be my slave for the rest of his life."

"Agreed," said the two friends. "But if you lose, what will you give us?"

"If I lose, I will divide my property in half, and give one-quarter of all that I own to each of you."

"As for me," said Wangchuk, "I will make the same bet. If I win, then you, Jigme, must give me half of everything you own; and Dersang, you will be my slave for the rest of your life. But if I lose, I will give one-quarter of my property to each of you." And the others also agreed to these terms.

"For my part," said Dersang, "I will make a wager also. If I win the hand of this beautiful girl, you each must give me half of everything you own. But if I fail, I will become a slave equally to each of you, and you may share my labor, and I will do all that you ask of me."

Having decided on the terms of their wager, the three young men agreed that they would settle their accounts after the whole contest was finished. Then each of them went home to prepare to seek the hand of the mysterious beautiful girl.

The next morning, Prince Jigme appeared at the door of the girl's house at the head of a great and magnificent parade. There were elephants draped with golden cloth, laden high with boxes of gifts that the prince took down and piled on the girl's doorstep. There were musicians and dancers who performed the most exquisite music to delight the girl's ears and eyes. Prince Jigme himself stood in front of the girl's house and delivered a long, passionate speech about how deeply in love he was with the mysterious girl and about all of the wonderful things that would be hers if she only would agree to be his princess.

Through all of this, the girl stayed in an inner room of her house, weaving at her loom and paying no attention at all to the fuss outside her door. She didn't even move the curtain aside from her window to peek out a single time. Finally, the prince's elephants were getting tired and cranky, the musicians and dancers had performed until they were ready to drop from fatigue, and Prince Jigme himself had long since lost his voice from proclaiming his undying love. Prince Jigme reluctantly realized that he had lost his bet, and he went back home to the palace, feeling very discouraged.

The next morning the street in front of the girl's house was crowded again, this time with dozens of servants from Wangchuk's house. Each servant was dressed in the finest silk clothing, and each carried some dazzling gift that had been brought from faraway kingdoms: ivory and jade, silver and gold, spices and sandalwood, silken cloth, and cloth of gold. One by one the servants piled the gifts on the girl's doorstep. Then Wangchuk began to recite a long poem that he had written, proclaiming in the most passionate terms his love for the mysterious girl. He was very handsome as well as being very rich, and he was dressed in his best robe of silk brocade, draped with diamonds and pearls. Altogether he was a sight that would have melted the heart of any other girl in the kingdom. But the object of his love simply kept on weaving at her loom and never glanced out the window at all. At the end of the day, Wangchuk admitted to himself that he had lost the bet, so he told his servants to pick up the gifts and go home.

The next morning Dersang walked slowly toward the home of the mysterious beautiful girl. He was dressed in a shabby old robe, with battered sandals on his feet; he looked almost like a beggar. He thought that there was no chance at all that the girl would pay any attention to him—let alone marry him—but he had agreed with his friends to be part of the wager, and so he thought it was his duty at least to try.

When he turned into the street where the girl lived, he saw an old granny coming his way. She looked at him shrewdly and said, "Sonny, if you are thinking of visiting the girl who lives in that house, you might as well forget about it. She never sees any males at all, and refuses to talk to them. It's pretty unlikely that she would make an exception for a beggar boy like you."

Then the boy began to get angry. "What's the matter with that girl, anyway?" he said to the old woman. "Is she crazy? Is she stupid? Is she deaf and mute? She must have some kind of serious problem to behave the way she does."

The old woman replied, "You don't know what you're talking about. My mistress—for in fact I am her old nursemaid and have served her since she was a child—is neither crazy, nor stupid, nor deaf and mute; on the contrary, she is exceptionally intelligent and well educated, in addition to being the most beautiful girl in the whole city. Her problem, I'm afraid, is quite a different one."

"Well, Grandmother," said the boy, "since you have told me

this much, you may as well tell me more. What is the problem with this girl that she is so hostile to males?"

"Her name is Drolma," said the old woman, "and it isn't really that she dislikes males, but rather that she remembers her previous lifetimes too well. She is so aware of everything that she suffered as a wife and mother in her previous lives that she is unwilling to go through that kind of pain and sorrow again."

"But what kind of sorrow can she have encountered to have had such a terrible effect on her?"

"For example," said the old woman, "in one lifetime Drolma had been born as a tigress, and she had three very sweet little tiger cubs. Her husband was a brave and fierce tiger, and they lived happily in the jungle together. But one day hunters came to the jungle and shot her three cubs with arrows. She tried to defend them, but there was nothing that she could do. Her husband heard her terrible cries and hurried back to where she and the cubs had been resting. A hunter shot again, and husband and wife fell dead, both of them pierced through the heart by a single arrow.

"Again, in another lifetime Drolma had been born as a plover, and she made her nest in a wheat field, where she laid three beautiful eggs. But the farmers chose just that time to burn off the stubble in their fields, and the flames threatened to destroy her nest and eggs and all. Drolma's husband flew to an irrigation ditch and wetted his wings, then flew back to the nest where he tried to save the eggs by fanning them with cool water. But his brave efforts came to nothing, and both the mother and the father bird were burned up along with their eggs.

"Yet another time she was reborn as a moorhen, and made her nest on a platform of reeds in a ditch by the side of the fields. But just then the farmers decided to release more water into the irrigation channels, and Drolma's nest was swept away. When she

and her husband tried to save the nest, they were both swept away
too and drowned.

"So you can see how Drolma's bad experiences in the past,
which she remembers as if they had happened in her own present
lifetime, have been so upsetting to her that she never wants to have
a husband and children again."

"Thank you, Grandmother, for telling me that very moving
story," said Dersang. "It surely will make me reflect deeply on the
meaning of karma." And he turned and walked away; but as soon
as the old woman had walked out of sight, he turned back again
and burst into the door of the beautiful girl's house.

"Darling, darling Drolma, my beloved wife, at last I've found
you after searching for you through many lifetimes," he cried,
flinging his arms around her, his voice choking with bitter tears.

"Help! Help!" screamed Drolma. "Who are you? Get out of
my house! Maids, maids, get this boy out of here!" she cried,
squirming out of his grasp and then trying to push him out the
door.

"Darling Drolma, don't you recognize me? I'm your husband, the very same husband who shared so many lifetimes with
you. We were separated a long time ago, and I've been searching
for you ever since, from one incarnation to the next. Now that I've
finally found you, you can't be so cruel as to push me out of your
house."

"How could you possibly be my husband? I don't recognize
you at all."

"But it's so strange. I recognized you at once. Still, I know
I can convince you of who I am. Do you remember, for example,
the time when we were incarnated as tigers? Our lives ended trag-
ically then, but think how cute our cubs were and how much we
loved them.

"And think, too, of that other time when we were plovers,

with our nest in the wheat fields. It was so sad when our eggs were destroyed in the fire."

"Yes, husband," said Drolma, looking more beautiful than ever, "I think I recognize you now. And I'm sure no one else could know about the things you're telling me. Husband, it was very brave of you to try to put out those flames by wetting your wings in the ditch."

"You were just as brave, my lovely wife," said Dersang, "when you were a moorhen and tried to save our nest as it was swept away in the irrigation channel."

"Oh, husband," said Drolma, "it is clear to me now that there is a strong karmic connection binding our lives together. I had been avoiding all males in this lifetime. I thought the reason was that I was trying to escape from the tragedies of life. But now I see that I was simply waiting here for you to find me. Let us fulfill our karma by getting married again at once."

"First come with me for a short while," said the orphan boy. "I would like you to meet my friends."

Dersang and Drolma walked together to the royal palace, where Prince Jigme came out to greet them. He could hardly believe his eyes.

"Allow me to introduce my wife," said Dersang. "And I believe you owe me one-half of all that you possess."

"I don't know how you did this," said the prince, "but I will pay it to you gladly, and I wish you both much happiness."

They went next to the house of Wangchuk, who stared at them in amazement. "I would like you to meet my wife," said Dersang, "and by the way, you owe me one-half of all that you possess."

"Of course. I will pay it to you at once. Someday, though, I hope you will at least tell me how you managed to pull this off. I am dying of curiosity. Meanwhile, best of luck to you both."

Dersang was now extremely wealthy. He built a beautiful palace for himself and his bride, and in just a few years they had three lovely children. They were very happy, and they often talked about the previous lives that they had shared together.

"WOW," SAID DERSANG, "that orphan boy was really smart!"

The moment the first word passed his lips, the leather strap broke and the sack burst open. Ngudup Dorjee flew out of the broken sack and gave Dersang a sharp slap on the cheek before he vanished into thin air.

The King's Heart

Dersang made his way back to Nagarjuna's cave, feeling exhausted and discouraged.

"I'm so sorry, Lord Nagarjuna," said the boy, "but he got away."

"He tricked you, did he?" said Nagarjuna.

"Yes, my lord," said Dersang. "He tricked me with a story."

"Well, Dersang," said Nagarjuna, "don't be too hard on yourself. He tricks everybody. He's very good at it. I've been trying for years to get hold of him so I can turn him into a lump of gold, and I haven't succeeded in doing it yet.

"In any case, you have shown yourself to be a brave and resourceful lad, as well as an honest one. I am going to accept you as my disciple. You will be known as Prince Dersang from now on. Your first task, until further notice, is to keep capturing Ngudup Dorjee until you succeed in bringing him back to me." And with that he gave Dersang another container of food, a new sack with a leather strap, and his old axe.

The next morning, Dersang left for the cemetery again, and after walking for several days through the forest, he arrived at the hillside cemetery. With some difficulty he found his way inside the cemetery walls (for the entryway kept changing, and one had to find a new path every time), and he found himself surrounded by hundreds of spirits.

"Where is Ngudup Dorjee?" shouted Dersang.

"Here, here, I am here," answered the spirits, with hundreds of voices all calling at once. But Dersang paid no attention to the spirits that answered him and watched carefully for a spirit that tried not to be seen.

Spotting Ngudup Dorjee hurrying away, Dersang pursued him, and soon Ngudup Dorjee climbed up a tall tree. "Ngudup Dorjee," Dersang called up to him, "come down from your tree, or I will chop the tree down." And Dersang took out his axe.

"That will not be necessary, boy," answered Ngudup Dorjee. "I'm coming down."

When Ngudup Dorjee had climbed down the tree, Dersang seized him by the neck, stuffed him into the sack, and tied it closed with the leather strap. It seemed to him that catching Ngudup Dorjee had been a bit easier this time.

Throwing the sack over his shoulder, Dersang left the cemetery and headed for the path through the deep dark forest back toward Nagarjuna's cave.

"It's a long, boring walk through the forest, boy," said Ngudup Dorjee from within the sack. "Why don't you tell a story to amuse us both along the way?"

Dersang of course did not reply, but just kept walking grimly ahead.

After a few more miles, Ngudup Dorjee again spoke from within the sack. "Well, boy, if you won't tell a story, I will."

Dersang of course did not want Ngudup Dorjee to tell a story, because he knew it would just be another trick, but he couldn't even say a single word to tell Ngudup Dorjee to be quiet. So he had to listen whether he wanted to or not; and this is what he heard:

ONCE, IN a certain country, there was a king who had one son, Crown Prince Rinchen. The king was old and in poor health, and the crown prince knew that it would soon be time for him to become king in his turn. He was not married and had no heir, so his parents were concerned that if anything happened to him the royal lineage would die out and the country would be in danger.

The crown prince was troubled by the heavy responsibilities that lay ahead of him. Sometimes, to escape from his worries, he would put on ordinary clothes and walk along the streets of his capital city; at such times no one recognized him as the crown prince.

One day, as he was walking through the city, he passed a small, poor-looking house where sitting by a window, weaving at her loom, was an extraordinarily beautiful young woman. Her name was Pema, and she was an orphan who lived alone in her small house with only an elderly maidservant to take care of her. Glancing out her window, she noticed the prince gazing at her with a troubled look on his face.

A moment later, without quite knowing why, Prince Rinchen knocked on the young woman's door, which she opened at once. Seeing the young man, Pema was filled with compassion for him.

"Sir, you seem troubled and sad," she said to him. "Would you like to have a cup of tea with me? Perhaps it would help you to rest and forget your worries for awhile."

"I would like that very much," said the prince, who felt that he was already falling in love with the beautiful young woman.

As they drank tea and talked together, it became clear to both of them that they must be bound by some strong karmic connection because before many minutes had passed they were deeply in love with one another. After tea, the prince stayed for supper, and after supper he stayed the night, rising from Pema's bed only just before dawn so that he could hurry back to the palace.

"Come back to see me again if you can," said the young woman.

"Of course," replied the prince. "I will never forget you."

The next night, and after that whenever he could leave the palace without being seen, the prince came to Pema's house and knocked at the door, and they spent many nights together sharing their secret love. During this time Pema became pregnant, and she was happy and proud to be bearing her lover's child.

Also during this time the old king died, and Crown Prince Rinchen became king in his turn. But this did not change at all the love that the young couple felt for one another, and King Rinchen continued to visit the young woman as often as he could.

One night he said to her, "My love, we have shared our nights and our love for several months now. My dearest wish is that you would marry me and be my wife forever."

"It makes me very happy that you ask that of me," said Pema, "but you know that I cannot accept your proposal. I realized long ago that you were the crown prince, and now you are the king. It is not at all suitable for you to marry a poor orphan girl like me; you must marry a princess from some neighboring country for the good of your own kingdom. I cannot marry you, but I will always love you."

It made King Rinchen very sad to hear his lover speak in this way, but he knew that she was right, so there was nothing he could say to change her mind. After some weeks had passed, he went to his mother, the widow of the old king, and said, "Mother, I think it is time for me to be married. Please select some suitable princess from a neighboring kingdom, and I will marry her and make her my queen."

The queen mother already had exactly the right princess in mind, so it took almost no time at all to make arrangements for the royal wedding. But as the day for the wedding approached, King Rinchen had a very frightening dream, and naturally he went to visit the one person who had always been able to comfort him in his worries and anxieties.

"I have had a terrible dream," he told Pema. "I dreamed that I got married, and immediately my spirit began to waste away within my body. In only a few weeks I was dead."

"Darling, that is a terribly upsetting dream," his lover said. "But sometimes dreams are just phantoms that mean nothing at all. I am confident that this dream is without significance. Please don't let it worry you. In any case, the date of your wedding is already set, and nothing can be done to change it. We must trust that the Lord Buddha will protect your life."

So the king got married in a grand ceremony attended by nobles and dignitaries from both countries. Naturally Pema, being a poor orphan, was not at the wedding, but like the rest of her countrymen she rejoiced in King Rinchen's good fortune and wished him a long and happy life.

About a month later, however, King Rinchen again knocked at the door of Pema's house. When she opened the door, she saw immediately that his entire appearance was transformed. His young healthy strength had gone: his chest was sunken, his cheeks were hollow, his skin was the color of ash. His eyes were clouded and dim, and his breathing was ragged and painful. He looked like a man on the verge of death.

"My darling, what has happened?" cried Pema.

"I'm afraid it is as the dream foretold," said the king. "The spirit is leaving my body, and I will die soon. I need your help now. Please come to the palace with me at once."

Pema put on a cloak and hurried with the king to the palace, though it was difficult for her to walk because she was so heavily pregnant. When they were inside the palace walls, he led Pema to the royal elephant stables, where she could rest on a bed of sweet straw in one of the empty stalls. "Listen," said the king. In the distance she could hear the sound of women's voices, screaming in anger. It was the queen mother quarreling with the new queen.

"Why have you done this to him?" screeched the queen mother. "Are you some kind of witch? You have stolen the sacred turquoise that King Rinchen always wore around his neck, and that is why his spirit is leaving his body. You are killing him."

"No, no, that's not true," the queen screamed back at her. "I love my husband. I never took his sacred turquoise; it just disappeared one day. I don't have any idea what happened to it."

"Witch! Monster! Liar!" screamed the queen mother. "It is not just his sacred turquoise that you have stolen. Other turquoise jewelry is also missing everywhere in the palace. What have you done with it. *Why* are you doing this? How can it benefit you to kill my son? Now the royal lineage will come to an end, and our country will be ruined."

"Actually, my mother is wrong," King Rinchen told Pema. "My wife is innocent; she has not stolen any jewelry. When I realized that I was dying, as my dream foretold, I took off the sacred turquoise myself and gathered up all of the other turquoise I could find and hid it to keep for you. It is hidden in a niche here in this elephant stable. I will show the place to you now; when I die, you must take it and use it to support yourself and our son. This is my last request to you: please take good care of my child. I have to return to my room now," said King Rinchen. "I will come back here again later if I can." He went back to the palace, and although his lover hoped that he would return, he did not.

Soon after he left, Pema felt the beginning of her labor pains. Fortunately her labor was easy and brief, and she gave birth to a healthy, beautiful son. When he was safely resting at her breast, she collapsed in a faint.

Early in the morning the elephant grooms came to the stable and immediately noticed that the elephants were restless and upset. Searching the stables for the cause of the great beasts' disquiet, they soon came upon the unconscious young woman, lying with her newborn on a blood-soaked pile of straw. Waking her up, they demanded to know who she was and what she was doing there. "I will explain everything," the young woman said, "but only to the queen mother. Please ask her to come here, for I have something very important to tell her."

The queen mother was informed and soon came to see the mysterious young woman. Impressed by her beauty and sincerity, the queen mother quickly stopped being angry at the outrage of a stranger giving birth in the royal stables, and she indicated that she would listen to the young woman's story.

"This baby boy is the son of the king," Pema confessed to the astonished queen mother. And she proceeded to tell the whole story of how she had become the king's secret lover. "And King Rinchen came to my house last night and brought me here to the royal stables. He told me that he had put together a treasure of turquoise so that I could always take good care of his child," Pema went on. "It is hidden here in one of the elephant stalls. Let me show you where it is."

As she was doing so, great cries of alarm and grief arose from within the palace. The servants had gone into the king's bedchamber to attend to his awakening and had discovered instead that he had died during the night. Quickly giving orders that the young woman and her baby were to be well cared for but prevented from leaving the palace, the queen mother went to see the body of her son.

Days passed while the lengthy and complicated ceremonies of the king's funeral were arranged and carried out. Finally, the queen mother came once again to see Pema and her son in the small palace room that had been set aside for them.

"It was wrong of you and the king to carry on a secret affair," said the queen mother, "but it has turned out very well in the end. I was very afraid that our royal line would die with the king, but it makes me very happy to know that he has a son to carry on after him. And I am pleased with your honesty in telling me about the missing turquoise. From that I know that you really were King Rinchen's lover and that your son is his son. You may continue to live here in the palace, and you will be treated as a junior widow of the king. As for your son, I will adopt him as my own. He will be king himself one day, and meanwhile I will rule as his regent."

And so it was.

One night a few weeks later, as Pema was sleeping in her room at the palace, she felt a strange disturbance in the room. Opening her eyes, she noticed the moonlight streaming in from the window, and she began to hear a strange tapping sound. Then she saw that her lover, King Rinchen, was standing near her bed, looking down at her. He looked pale and ghostly and was wearing the same clothes in which he had been buried. "My darling, I have come back to see you," he said. "Tell me, how is our son?"

"As you see, our son is well," she replied, pointing to the beautiful little boy in his cradle. "Please wait a moment while I call your mother to see you also. She misses you terribly, and I know that she would want very much to see you now that you have returned from the dead."

"No," said King Rinchen, "you cannot do that. I have found my way back to you only with great difficulty. If you leave the room now to call my mother, I also will have to flee from this place, and I don't know if I will be able to return. Let me just stay here with you for awhile." So the late king stayed in his lover's room, sharing the night as they had so many times in the past.

While they were talking together, Pema thought, "Let me at least keep something to show the queen mother, so that she will know that her son's visit was real and that I was not merely dreaming." And without his noticing it, she took the sash from King Rinchen's robe and placed it under her sleeping son in his cradle.

As dawn approached, King Rinchen prepared to leave again, to return to the land of the dead. "Where is my sash?" he asked.

"I have put it in the cradle," she replied. "If you try to take it out now, I'm afraid you will wake our son and make him cry. Maybe it would be better if you just left it behind."

"That's fine," he replied. "I must go now. I will come again if I can."

That morning Pema told the queen mother all about her son's visit. At first the queen mother did not believe her, but when she saw the sash from her son's robe, the very same one that he was wearing when he was buried, she knew that her daughter-in-law was telling the truth. The queen mother was glad to hear that her son had been able to come back from the land of the dead, even for a short time, but she was also upset that she had not been able to see him. "If he comes again, you must find a way to inform me, so that I can talk with him also," she said.

"I will try, Your Majesty," the young woman replied.

"Please try," she said. "I want so much to see my son again."

A month later, the king again came to visit his lover, coming into her room with the light of the full moon. Suddenly she realized that he was standing beside her bed, and she welcomed him back. "But please, this time, my love," she said, "let me send word to your mother also. She is so eager to see you. My heart feels very sad for her that you are so near to her now and she cannot see you."

"I am very sorry to say this," said King Rinchen, "but now I can only come back from the dead to see you. I am dead, but not completely dead; your love for me is keeping me from disappearing in death altogether. But I am afraid that if I were to try to see anyone else, I would never be able to return again."

"Is there nothing at all to be done?" she asked. "I have come to love your mother very much, and I would do anything to make her happy."

"There may be a way for my mother to see me again," said King Rinchen, "but it would be very dangerous for you, and you might very well die. I can't bear the thought of putting you in such danger."

"No, if there is a way, then we must try," she replied. "Now my life seems very empty, but if I could help your mother, that would be very meaningful to me."

"In that case, I will tell you what you must do," said her lover. "It is very difficult and dangerous.

"At the next new moon, the last night of the lunar month, when the sky will be dark all night, you must go on a long journey. Before dark, prepare to take with you what you will need: a piece of bone and two pieces of cloth wrapped in a bundle," he said. "When darkness falls, leave the palace and walk straight to the west. You will walk all night through a deep, dark forest, full of mysterious lights and sounds, full of strange creatures that you have never seen before. You will be surrounded by dangers on all sides, but you must keep walking westward all night, until near dawn you will emerge from the forest at the borders of a strange country. Continue walking straight ahead.

"Soon you will come to a beautiful pond. It will be full of

clear water, with fish and ducks swimming in the water and birds
flying and singing nearby; the banks will be covered with lovely
green plants bursting with flowers. As you walk past it, you must
say, 'I have seen many ponds in my life, and this is the ugliest pond
that I have ever seen.' And then you will continue walking.

"In a few miles you will come to anther pond. This pond will
be extremely ugly. Its water will be brown with mud and pollution, and it will smell like a sewer. No fish will live in the water,
and no ducks will swim in it, nor will any birds sing nearby. Its
banks will be muddy and rocky, with no sign of any living plants.
When you reach this pond, you must pause and drink a handful
of its water, and then you will say, 'In my life I have seen many
ponds, but I have never seen a pond as beautiful as this one, and I
have never tasted such delicious, refreshing water.' And you will
continue walking.

"After awhile you will come to a stupa. It will be a very beautiful stupa, made of dazzling white marble inlaid with precious
stones, and surrounding it will be a lovely garden full of fountains
and flowers. As you walk past, you must say, 'In my life I have seen
many stupas, but I have never seen another stupa as ugly as this
one.' And you will continue walking.

"In a few more miles you will come to another stupa. This
one will be exceptionally ugly, made of mud and dung, neglected
by everyone, half falling down, surrounded by bare dirt and a
ruined garden full of dead plants. At this stupa you must pause to
bow down and pray, and when you have finished your prayers you
must say, 'In my life I have seen many stupas, but I have never
seen another stupa as beautiful as this one.'

"As you walk along further, you will see two dogs fighting
over a bone. When you reach them, take out the bone that you
have brought with you in your bundle and give it to one of the
dogs. You should say, 'Please stop fighting, dogs. Now there is a

bone for each of you.' They will stop fighting, and you will continue walking.

"After a few miles, you will see two boys fighting over a
piece of cloth. One of them will be wearing the cloth, and the
other, nearly naked, will be trying to take the cloth away. Take out
one of the pieces of cloth that you have brought with you in your
bundle and give it to the naked boy and say, 'Please stop fighting.
Now there is a cloth for each of you.' And they will stop fighting,
and you will continue on your way.

"Soon you will see by the side of the road an old woman who
has been selling toasted barley. She has sold all of it and needs to
clean out the pan in which she has been toasting the barley. But
she is too poor to have even a rag to wipe out her pan, so instead
she has taken out one of her own big, drooping breasts and is wiping the pan with it. Give her your second piece of cloth and say
to her, 'Grandmother, it is not right that you should use your own
breast to wipe out this pan. Please take this piece of cloth that I
have brought for you.' And she will thank you, and you will continue on your way.

"At last you will come to the gate of a big palace. The gate
will be guarded, but do not pay any attention to the guards; you
may walk right past them and enter the palace. As you enter the
gate, you will see many courtyards and gardens, but do not pay
attention to them. Just continue walking until you have made
your way to the very center of the palace.

"When you arrive there, you will see a big room with many
people in it, all dressed in strange costumes. They will be facing
the center of the room. There, in the middle of the floor, will be
inlaid in stones a pattern of nine squares. In each of the eight outer
squares, you will see a large heart, still beating although it is not
contained in any body. In the center square, you will also see a
small heart, still beating. You must enter the room and take this

small heart from the center square. When you have taken it, quickly return back here to your own home. If you are able to do all of this, I think that my circumstances will become much better, and I will be able to see my mother again." By this time it was almost dawn, and King Rinchen then had to leave his lover's room once again to return to the land of the dead.

The next morning, Pema told the queen mother that her son had visited her again in the night and had given her instructions to go on a long journey. Then she prepared a bundle with a piece of bone and two pieces of cloth and patiently waited until the last night of the lunar month, when the sky would be dark all night.

When the night of the new moon came, Pema left the palace at nightfall and made her way straight westward on a path that led through the great western forest. The forest was full of strange lights and frightening noises, and she could hear the rustling of wild beasts all around her, but she paid no attention to any of those things and just walked all night until she came out of the forest on the borders of a strange land. Then everything occurred just as her lover said it would.

First she came to a beautiful pond. It was full of clear water, with fish and ducks swimming in the water and birds flying and singing nearby; the banks were covered with lovely green plants bursting with flowers. As she walked past it, she said, "I have seen many ponds in my life, and this is the ugliest pond that I have ever seen." And she continued on her way.

In a few miles she came to another pond. This pond was extremely ugly. Its water was brown with mud and pollution, and it smelled like a sewer. No fish lived in the water, and no ducks swam in it, nor were any birds singing nearby. Its banks were muddy and rocky and devoid of living plants. When she reached this pond, she paused as she was told to do and drank a handful of its water, and then said, "In my life I have seen many ponds, but

I have never seen a pond as beautiful as this one, and I have never tasted such delicious, refreshing water." And she kept on walking.

After awhile she came to a stupa. It was a very beautiful stupa, made of dazzling white marble inlaid with precious stones, surrounded by a lovely garden full of fountains and flowers. As she walked past, she said, "In my life I have seen many stupas, but I have never seen another stupa as ugly as this one." And she continued on her way.

In a few more miles she came to another stupa. This one was exceptionally ugly, made of mud and dung, neglected by everyone, half falling down, surrounded by bare dirt and a ruined garden full of dead plants. At this stupa she paused to bow down and pray, and after she had finished praying she said, "In my life I have seen many stupas, but I have never seen another stupa as beautiful as this one." And she continued walking.

Further on, she saw two dogs fighting over a bone. When she reached them, she took out the bone she had brought with her and gave it to one of the dogs. She said, "Please stop fighting, dogs. Now there is a bone for each of you." The dogs stopped fighting, and Pema kept on walking.

After a few miles, she saw two boys fighting over a piece of cloth. One of them was wearing the cloth, and the other, nearly naked, was trying to take the cloth away. She took out one of the pieces of cloth that she brought with her and gave it to the naked boy. She said, "Please stop fighting. Now there is a cloth for each of you." They stopped fighting, and Pema continued on her way.

Soon she saw by the side of the road an old woman who was selling toasted barley. She had sold all of it, and she needed to clean out the pan in which she had been toasting the barley. But she was too poor to have even a rag to wipe out her pan, so instead she took out one of her own big, drooping breasts and was wiping the pan with it. Pema gave her the second piece of cloth, and said to her,

"Grandmother, it is not right that you should use your own breast to wipe out this pan. Please take this piece of cloth that I have brought for you." The old woman thanked her, and she continued on her way.

At last she came to the gate of a big palace. The gate was guarded, but she did not pay any attention to the guards; she walked right past them and entered the palace. As she entered the gate, she saw many courtyards and gardens, but she paid no attention to them and just continued walking until she made her way to the very center of the palace.

When she arrived there, she saw a big room with many people in it. All dressed in strange costumes, they were facing the center of the room. There, in the middle of the floor, was inlaid in stones a pattern of nine squares. In each of the eight outer squares, she saw a large heart, still beating although it was not contained in any body. In the center square, she also saw a small heart, still beating.

Feeling very frightened, Pema entered the room in the center of the palace. She only hesitated for a moment before she rushed past the people crowding around the room and seized the small heart in the centermost square of the pattern inlaid in the stone floor. Immediately she turned around again and ran out of the room.

The king of that country, who was one of the strangely dressed people in the room, ran after her, shouting for the guards to close the gates of the palace. But she was too quick for them; before they could move the heavy gates enough to close them completely, she had slipped through the door and was running along the road away from the palace.

Chasing her, the king saw an old woman sitting by the roadside up ahead. "Stop her! Stop that woman," he cried.

But the old woman said to him, "This kingdom is so poor

and miserable that I didn't even have a rag to wipe out my cooking pot and had to clean it with my own poor sagging breast. This young woman helped me by giving me a piece of cloth to use, and I will do nothing to harm her."

Then the king saw two boys on the road ahead, just where the young woman was running to get away from him. "Stop her! Stop her! Don't let her get away!" the king shouted.

But the boys replied, "Here we live in a land so cruel and so badly ruled that one of us was naked, and we were fighting over a piece of cloth. This young woman gave us another piece, so we could both be clothed; we will do nothing to harm her." And the woman ran past them, pursued by the king.

Next the king saw two dogs on the road ahead and called to them, "Stop her! I will reward you if you do not let her get away."

But the dogs also said, "We were fighting over an old bone, and this young woman gave us another bone so we each could have one and would no longer need to fight. We will do nothing to harm her." And Pema ran past, pursued by the king.

Then the king saw a stupa up ahead, and called out, "Stupa! Use your magic power to prevent that woman from getting past you."

But the stupa replied, "For many, many years people have considered me too ugly and decrepit to be worth bothering with. But this young woman showed me respect by calling me beautiful and bowing down to pray in front of me. Since I have existed in this place, this young woman is the only person who has ever shown respect to me. I will do nothing to harm her." So the woman escaped again.

Soon the king saw another stupa ahead and again he called, "Stupa! Use your magic power to prevent that woman from getting past you."

But the stupa replied, "Everyone has always said that I am

the most beautiful stupa in the kingdom, but this young woman showed me no respect at all and said I was the ugliest stupa she had ever seen. She must have some very powerful force protecting her in order to speak so boldly. I am afraid of her and will not take the risk of impeding her escape." So the woman ran on toward the borders of the kingdom.

Seeing a pond near the road ahead where the woman was running, the king called out, "Pond! Use your floodlike power to prevent this young woman from escaping."

But the pond replied, "For as long as I can remember, I have been scorned and neglected because people consider me ugly. But this young woman respected me; she said that I am beautiful, and she drank some of my water and called it delicious. She is the only person who has ever shown me such respect. I will do nothing to harm her." And the woman continued running past the pond.

Again the king saw another pond ahead and he cried, "Pond! Use your floodlike power to prevent this young woman from escaping."

But the pond replied, "Everyone has always said that I am the most beautiful pond in the kingdom. But this young woman was not impressed by my beauty; indeed she said that I am the ugliest pond she had ever seen. She must be protected by some powerful force to speak so boldly. I am afraid of her, and I will do nothing to arouse her anger at me." So she passed the last obstacle and finally was able to escape from the king.

When she passed the last pond, Pema arrived at the border between the strange kingdom and the deep forest. When she entered the forest path, the king who had been pursuing her stopped, and it was evident that some power prevented him from going farther. So she was safe, and she returned through the forest to her own palace without any more danger or difficulty.

Late that night, as she was sleeping in her own room in the

palace, Pema again heard a tapping at the window. Waking up, she saw King Rinchen standing next to her bed. But he no longer looked like someone who had suffered a terrible illness and died; instead he was restored to his old health and beauty. "Now you may take me to see my mother," he said, "because you have restored me to life. You have been to the land of the dead, and the beating heart that you recovered is my own heart, which is now beating in my chest once again. Thanks only to you, I am able to be restored to my mother, and to my wife, and to you, the mother of my son."

Then they went to the rooms of the queen mother, who was overjoyed to see King Rinchen restored to life and good health. And when she heard what the young woman had done to bring this about, she said, "You also shall be my son's wife, and you and his other wife the queen will live as sisters. Your son will be the crown prince, and may he long enjoy the love and protection of his father."

And so it was. King Rinchen lived and reigned for many years, and he treated both of his wives with love and consideration. He was respectful to his mother and kind to his son (and to his many other children as well), and everyone in his kingdom felt very fortunate to live under the reign of such a ruler.

"WHAT AN amazing girl, to bring back a heart from the land of the dead," said Dersang. And the leather strap broke, the sack burst open, and Ngudup Dorjee once again gave Dersang a slap on the cheek before flying back to his home in the cemetery.

The Carpenter Who Went
to Heaven

Once upon a time, there was a certain kingdom ruled by a king who was both wise and good. But although the king was not very old, he fell ill and soon passed away. Thereupon his son, the crown prince, became king in his turn.

The new king, however, was good but not wise; in fact, he was slightly simple-minded, and it was easy for others to take advantage of him.

Among the citizens of the king's capital city were a carpenter and a house-painter. They often worked together, but they were not friends. This is because the house-painter was an angry, mean-spirited man who felt very jealous of the carpenter's skill at his work and also of the carpenter's easy, friendly manner that made him popular with all the other people in town.

When the king died, and the new king took the throne, the house-painter saw that his chance had finally arrived to get rid of his rival. One day, he dressed himself up in a long white robe, powdered his face and arms with chalk so that they were a ghostly white, put a garland of flowers around his neck and a crown of flowers in his hair, and walked up the main street of the town to the gates of the palace. Soon he was followed by a great crowd of people who were curious about this strange-looking being in their midst, and the crowd made so much noise that the king heard them from the palace window.

Leaning out the window, the king called to the creature in white, "Who are you, and what do you want?"

"I have come from heaven to report to you," said the strange being.

"Come in," said the king, "and let me hear what you have to say."

The creature in white was let into the palace and brought into the royal audience room, where the king by that time was sitting on his golden throne.

"Have you really come from heaven?" asked the king.

"Indeed I have," said the ghostly being, "and I bring you a message from your father."

"My father? Are you saying that you've seen my father since he died? Is he well?"

"Yes, he is. He is very happy, and he looks better than he has in years. He is enjoying being in heaven with all of his ancestors and aunts and uncles. But he sent me here to see you especially because he has a request to make."

"What is his request? I would do anything at all to make my father happy."

"His request is this. There are so many members of your family in heaven that their small house there has become overcrowded. Your father intends to build a spacious and comfortable new house in heaven for all of his relatives. But in order to do this, he needs a carpenter, so he is asking you to send a carpenter up to heaven for him."

"Well, it happens that we have an excellent carpenter here in town," said the king, "and I'd be very happy to send him to heaven to serve my father. But I must say, I've never heard of such a thing before. How would he get there?"

"It's quite easy," said the house-painter in disguise. "You simply need to build a big pile of firewood in your garden, ask the carpenter to sit on top of it, and light the wood with a torch. The carpenter will be borne up to heaven on the smoke."

"I can see how that might work," said the king. "I'll see to it right away."

As soon as the ghostly figure had left the palace and wandered away down the main street, the king summoned the carpenter to the audience hall.

"Carpenter," said the king, "I have an unusual job for you. My late father, the king, wishes to build a new royal palace in heaven, and he has asked specifically for your services. I am going to send you up to heaven to work for him."

"I'm flattered, Your Majesty," said the carpenter, "but how will I get to heaven? I've never heard of anyone doing that before."

"It's simple," said the king. "We'll just build a big pyre of wood in the garden, have you sit on top, and light a fire. You'll drift up to heaven with the smoke."

"Excuse me, Your Majesty," said the carpenter, "but are you sure that will work? It sounds dangerous."

"Nonsense," said the king. "This is exactly how the heavenly messenger instructed that we should do it. But in any case, you should realize that I am not *asking* you to go work for my father in heaven, I am *ordering* you to go. I want you back here at the palace just as soon as I tell you that my workmen have finished building the bonfire."

"As you command, Your Majesty," said the carpenter. And he left the audience hall and walked home feeling very sad and frightened.

Now it happened that the carpenter's wife was an unusually smart and clever woman, and as soon as her husband came home, she realized that there was something terribly wrong. "What is the matter, my dear husband?" she asked.

The carpenter told her the whole story and added, "I'm afraid it's all over for us. When the king orders the fire to be lit, I will surely die, and then I'll never see you again." And he began to weep.

"Don't give up yet," said his wife. "I recognize this as some evil scheme of that nasty man, the house-painter. But I have thought of a way to save your life. You must go back to the palace again and speak to the king. . . ."

FOLLOWING HIS wife's instructions, the carpenter went back to the palace and asked to speak to the king, who was quite happy to see him.

"Your Majesty," said the carpenter, "I am honored to be invited to heaven to work for the late king, but I'm afraid that if I left from your garden I might lose my way because it all would seem so unfamiliar to me. I ask permission to leave from my own garden instead."

"That seems reasonable," said the king. "I'll send some workers to your house tomorrow to help build the pyre."

The carpenter returned home, and he and his wife immediately began to work frantically to dig a tunnel connecting their garden and the innermost room of the house. They worked all night and finally finished the job. The next morning, as the workmen arrived to build the pyre, they found that the carpenter and his wife had already made a big circular pile of logs out in the yard, a safe distance from the house.

"I'll just stand here, inside this ring of logs," said the carpenter. "Keep piling on more wood, and when there's enough you can light the fire."

The workers figured that a carpenter should know all about how to make a wood fire, so they followed his directions. They piled the logs higher and higher, adding plenty of green wood and leaves so that there would be a lot of smoke. Finally everything was ready, and a big crowd gathered to watch the carpenter go to heaven. The house-painter showed up, too, and saying that he would be happy to have the honor of helping his fellow construction worker in such an honorable and wonderful affair, he thrust a torch into the pile of logs and the fire blazed up.

Standing inside the ring of logs, the carpenter waited until there was a lot of smoke to disguise what he was doing; then he kicked aside the mat covering the entrance to the tunnel, climbed down into it, and made his way into his house. Meanwhile a big cloud of smoke rose to heaven, and everyone was sure that the carpenter had been carried upward with the smoke. Certainly no trace was left of him, and the house-painter went home feeling very satisfied at how he had gotten rid of his rival.

Afterward, the carpenter stayed within his house for a whole month, not daring to go outside or to risk being seen by anyone. His wife brought him his meals, and he even began to get a little bit fat from sitting around doing nothing but eating. He lost his usual dark suntan, and his whole appearance was quite different from before.

Then, after an entire month had passed, he was ready to return to the world. He put on his best clothes and walked to the gates of the palace, where he waited for the king to have his morning audience.

Finally he was shown into the presence of the king, who was

rather surprised to see him. The king greeted him with great friendliness and respect. "Well, carpenter," he said, "what news do you bring me of my father in heaven?"

"The news is very good, Your Majesty," said the carpenter. "I had a very safe and smooth trip up to heaven, and I immediately began working with your father, the late king, to design and build his new palace. We had an abundant supply of the finest wood and plenty of heavenly assistants to act as helpers, so we were able to complete the palace in just one month. It is very beautiful, and your father is very pleased with it.

"He sent me back down to earth now, because my part of the job is finished. But he does have another request for you."

"Oh?" said the king, "and what is that?"

"He needs a house-painter."

SO THE very next day the house-painter was ordered to sit on a big wooden pyre in the king's garden, and when the wood was set on fire maybe he went up to heaven with the smoke. Nobody knows for sure, but anyway, he was never seen in the king's city again.

The Woodcutter
and His Son

Once there was a poor woodcutter who lived with his son in a small house near a big forest. The woodcutter and his son would go into the forest every day to cut wood, which they sold to people for firewood. It was very hard work cutting and carrying the wood, and they did not make much money. But they were content with their fate in life.

The woodcutter was an ordinary, ignorant man with a terrible temper, but in spite of his faults, the son loved his father very much. The son himself was not very bright, but he lived a simple life that did not make many demands on his mind. So the father and son got along quite well together, and the years went by.

As the father began to get old, the son worried whether he would be able to do the hard, heavy work of a woodcutter for much longer. Sometimes the son would say to him, "Father, you should stay home and rest today. I will go to the forest and do enough work for both of us. Why don't you stay home and make a nice meal for the two of us to eat when I have finished working?"

Really, the son could not do as much work as the two of them together, so when he worked alone they made even less money than before. But the son felt that he was doing the right thing by making life easier for his father.

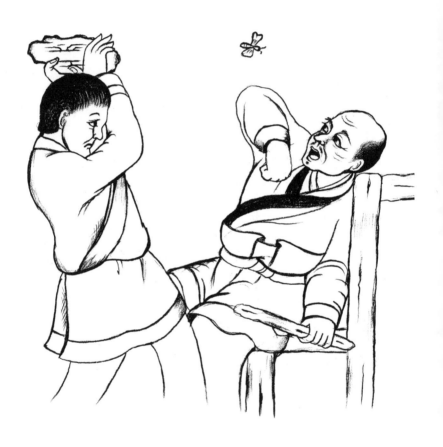

So it was that one day, the father stayed home to cook while the son worked in the forest. The father was standing at the stove pouring some oil into a frying pan. Afterward, he put the stopper back into the mouth of the oil jar and started to put it away. As usual in that part of the world, the oil jar had a small loop of rope around its neck so that it could be hung from a nail on the wall of the kitchen. So the father reached up to hang the jar on its nail— or at least what he thought was its nail. But he was getting old, and his eyesight was not so good anymore, and what he thought was a nail was just a little fly resting on the kitchen wall. The old man stretched his arm to hang up the jar and then let go as the fly went buzzing away. Of course, the jar came crashing down and smashed to pieces, spilling oil all over the floor.

When the old man realized what had happened, he lost his temper completely. "Fly," he said, "this is all your fault. Now I will kill you for sure." Looking around the room, he saw a small dark spot on the wall, which he was sure was the fly. Walking slowly and stealthily across the room, he slammed his fist as hard as he could against the wall. Unfortunately, the dark spot really was a nail this time, and it plunged deep into the old man's hand, making a painful, jagged wound from which blood poured onto the floor.

Just then, the son came home from the forest. "Father, what's happened?" the son cried. "Why are you bleeding so badly from your hand?"

"A nasty, sneaky fly has injured my hand," the father said, "besides breaking the oil jar and ruining all the cooking oil."

"Any fly that does that to my father must die," thought the son. So after he bandaged up his father's hand, he went outside to find a heavy stone that would fit comfortably into his hand. He'd make sure the fly would not get away this time.

When the son entered the house again, he saw that the fly

was back on the kitchen wall. The son slammed the rock in his hand against the wall where the fly was resting, but the fly flew away. All the blow did was to knock down some other jars that had been hanging from nails on the wall. Then the fly landed on the window. *Smash!* went the rock, and broken glass flew everywhere.

Little by little the son was knocking down their whole house, but all he noticed was the fly. Meanwhile the father kept calling out, "Good shot! Nice try! You almost got him that time!"

Finally, the fly landed on the father's head. "Hold still, father," said his son. And *smash!* The rock struck the father's head, and he fell down in a pool of blood.

"What have I done?" thought the son. "I tried to kill the fly that had made my father angry, but it seems that I have killed my father instead."

The fly buzzed as it flew across the room.

How Norbu Became a King

"You must learn to concentrate, Dersang," said Lord Nagarjuna. "That's what mindfulness means. You can't let yourself be distracted by nonessentials. Your task is to bring Ngudup Dorjee back to the cave. He will try to distract you with a story. You already know that is going to happen. So you must learn to concentrate your mind."

"I know, Lord Nagarjuna," replied Dersang, sadly. "But he's very tricky. His stories confuse my mind, and I forget what I'm supposed to be doing."

"Well, the time has come for you to try again," the sage said. "You've rested for long enough; now you must be off to the old cemetery again. I've prepared a fresh container of special food for your long trip and a new bag and strap, and here is your axe."

"Goodbye, Lord Nagarjuna," called Dersang as he left the cave. "I'll try very hard this time."

After walking for a few days, Dersang came to the old cemetery again and found his way inside. "Where is Ngudup Dorjee?" he cried.

"Here, here, I'm over here," replied hundreds of voices in all directions. But Dersang kept a sharp eye out, and he saw a dim shape slinking off while all of the other spirits were calling out to him. Following right on Ngudup Dorjee's trail, he soon chased him up a tree.

"Ngudup Dorjee, I am going to chop your tree down if you don't climb down at once," shouted Dersang.

"No, no, that won't be necessary. I'll come down," said Ngudup Dorjee. And as soon as he was within reach as he climbed down from the tree, Dersang grabbed him by the scruff of his neck, threw him into the sack, and pulled the leather strap tight.

As he walked back through the forest toward home, Dersang reminded himself to say nothing at all, no matter what Ngudup Dorjee might say.

"Boy, it's your turn to tell a story," said Ngudup Dorjee from inside the sack. "It's not fair that I have to be the only storyteller around here."

Dersang said nothing.

"Do you mean to say that you don't know any stories?" said Ngudup Dorjee, mockingly. "What kind of a boy are you, anyway?"

Dersang said nothing.

"Well, somebody has to tell a story on this long trip," said Ngudup Dorjee, "so I suppose it has to be me. I think you will like this one."

ONCE UPON A TIME, there was a small kingdom where almost all of the people were farmers. The valley where they lived did not get very much rain, so all of the farmers depended on irrigation to water their crops. There was a large pond that they used to supply their water. Every spring, they would cut a ditch through the bank of the pond and allow water to flow out into the irrigation channels; then they would fill up the ditch in the rim of the pond with mud to stop the flow of water.

Unfortunately, in the pond there lived two very fierce *naga*s, a male and a female, who year after year would capture and eat the man who dug the ditch into the bank of their pond. Everyone in the kingdom understood that this would happen every year, but they had no choice but to depend on the pond for their irrigation. So every year, in order to raise their crops, one man had to die.

Of course, no one wanted the job of digging the ditch into the bank of the pond, so the people devised a way of assigning the job in a way that everyone agreed was fair. Every year, in the early spring before planting time, every man in the entire kingdom had to play a game of dice. Everyone paired off with someone else, and they threw the dice. The losers dropped out of the game, but the winners went on to the next round and played again. That way, half of the men were eliminated from the game each time until there were only two men left. They threw the dice again. The "loser" was really the winner, because he got to remain alive, and the "winner" was really the loser, because he surely would be killed by the *naga*s after he had finished digging the ditch at the edge of the pond.

No one was exempt from playing the game. Every adult male, even the king and his family, had to play every year. And one year it happened that the king's only son won the last round of dice, and so he became the unlucky man who would have to dig the ditch and be killed by the *naga*s. The king and queen were devastated by this turn of events, but they understood that they could do nothing about it because the dice game was completely fair and everyone had abided by its results for as long as anyone could remember. And everyone in the kingdom was sad also because the prince was a generous, handsome, young man, and he was very popular.

However, it happened that in the same kingdom there was a very poor family consisting of an old man, his wife, and their grown-up son, Norbu. They were honest and hardworking, but it seemed that they were always poor; they never had enough to eat or proper clothes to wear, and the house they lived in was hardly more than a shack. When he heard the news about the prince's fate, Norbu said to himself, "It is very sad that the prince will have to die like that. I don't know if it is possible for there to be a substitute for the person chosen to dig the ditch, but perhaps it might be. Maybe I could take his place. I don't worry about dying because everyone dies. I only worry about my aged parents. But if the king would agree to take care of them after I'm gone, I would not have to worry about them either. Surely the prince's life is worth more than mine. If I die, hardly anyone will care, but if he dies, the whole kingdom will suffer. It would certainly be a good thing if I took his place."

So Norbu went to the royal palace and told the king about his idea. At first the king was shocked that anyone would volunteer to die in such a way, but of course he was also happy that there might be a way to save the life of his son.

Norbu said to the king, "If I agree to substitute for your son, the prince, you must also agree to do something for me. You must promise to take good care of my parents. They have been poor all their lives; you must make them comfortable now. And when they get old and die, you must establish a charitable foundation in their name so that they can continue to get religious merit in their future incarnations."

"I will promise to do all of that," said the king, "and I appoint you the royal substitute for my son, the prince. Thank you very much for saving his life."

The next day, Norbu said goodbye to his parents and, taking his shovel and his hoe, climbed the hill to the pond and began to dig. It was hard work and took several hours; it was dark by the time he had finished. But when the work was done, he sat down on the bank of the pond and waited for the *naga*s to come for him. He expected to feel their sharp teeth and claws at any moment, but for a long time nothing happened. So after awhile he couldn't stay awake any longer, so he put his head down and fell asleep.

He woke up at dawn, and at first he thought he must have been killed and eaten and that his soul was already in the next world. But he soon realized that he was just sitting on the bank of the pond, same as before, and the world was waking up around him. He heard the croaking of frogs and the buzzing of insects, and soon he realized that he could also make out two strange, hissing voices speaking in actual words. He crept forward to get a closer look and saw that a turtle was talking angrily to someone else, but he couldn't see who it was. "It's all your fault," said the turtle. "You let him get away."

Then Norbu looked up and saw that a tree had a small knothole partway up its trunk, and as he watched, a small snake slithered out of the hole and down the tree.

"And where were you last night?" the snake hissed at the turtle. "I was waiting for you so that we could have our meal together, but you never showed up."

"Why did you wait for me?" answered the turtle. "What was it to you if I was busy? Now it is already dawn, and we have lost the chance to kill and eat this person. I'm afraid he will get away."

"I waited for you out of simple politeness. You could have let me know if you were going to be late or weren't going to show up at all. I could have killed him and saved him for both of us," replied the snake.

As Norbu listened, the snake and the turtle became more and more angry with each other. He realized that they were in fact the *naga*s of the pond, transformed into the shape of ordinary water animals during the hours of daylight. Now they were becoming more and more angry with each other and were on the verge of fighting.

"How could you be so stupid as to let him get away?" said the turtle. "I'm angry enough to kill you myself."

"I'll kill you first," hissed the snake. "Don't think I wouldn't."

"If you kill me, there's a secret that you'll miss out on," replied the turtle, growing more and more angry. "So I'll be dead and you won't know what to do with my body."

"You're wrong about that," said the snake. "I know all about your secret. After I've killed you, I'll wrap your body in a five-colored silk cloth, and your corpse will turn into a pile of jewels— diamonds and rubies and sapphires. I know your secret, all right, but if you kill me, you would have no idea what to do with my body."

"Don't be so sure of that," said the turtle. "When I kill you, I'll wash your body and swallow it whole. Then whenever I hiccup or vomit, whatever liquid comes out of my mouth will immediately turn to gold."

The snake and the turtle went on like that, arguing and threatening each other, but Norbu had heard enough. Picking up his hoe, he killed both the snake and the turtle on the spot. He didn't have any five-colored silk, but he wrapped the turtle in an ordinary cloth and put it into his shoulder-bag. And the body of the snake he washed and swallowed whole. Very soon he began to hiccup, and the saliva that he spat out turned to lumps of pure gold. Feeling very pleased to be alive, he walked back to town and went to the king's palace.

The king was very surprised to see Norbu alive, and at first he wondered if Norbu had failed to go to the pond to dig the irrigation ditch as he had promised to do. But when he heard the whole story, he was very happy that Norbu had managed to come out of his experience alive and that the evil *naga*s of the pond were apparently gone forever. Norbu gave the body of the turtle to the king and told him to wrap it in a five-colored silk cloth, and sure enough, it turned into a big heap of diamonds and rubies and sapphires. And Norbu and his parents became quite rich because he could get gold whenever he wanted it by hiccupping it up.

Norbu also became close friends with the prince whose life he had saved. As the years went by, they remained good companions and often did things together. And with the passage of time, Norbu's parents passed away, and so did the king and the queen, and the prince became king in his turn.

Not long after that, Norbu and the young king were feeling rather depressed because they both missed their parents. There was nothing they felt like doing in the palace or in the town. "Let's go over the mountain pass to the next valley and go camping," suggested Norbu. The king thought that was a good idea, so before long they set out together.

When they got to the valley, they noticed a very large crowd of people milling about in the distance, apparently holding some kind of festival. They naturally went over to see what was happening, and they soon saw that a large elephant was rushing here and there among the crowd, holding a water jar in its trunk. As Norbu and the king watched, the elephant approached them and gently placed the water jar on the king's head. At once the crowd began cheering and roaring with pleasure. "Our king! Our king! The elephant has crowned our new king," they all shouted. Then they surrounded the king, picked him up, and put him on the back of the elephant; the elephant and everyone in the crowd went rushing off. Norbu had been ignored in all of this, and soon he was left standing alone in the middle of the big valley.

Not wanting to go back home because he was too unhappy to want to explain to the people there how their king had been taken away, Norbu began walking toward a small hill on the side of the valley, in the distance. When he got there, he saw a small house built up against the hillside. Because he was hungry and thirsty and had no place to go, he knocked on the door of the house, and it was opened by a beautiful young woman.

"Could you please give me some food and drink and a place to spend the night?" asked Norbu.

"Maybe, but first I have to ask my mother," said the girl. And she went inside again to where her mother was working in the kitchen.

"Mother, there is a man outside who wants food and drink and a place to spend the night," said the daughter.

"That's fine," the mother replied. "But he can't expect these things for free. Ask him if he can pay."

The girl asked Norbu if he had money, and he answered, "Yes, I have plenty of gold."

"Come in then," said the girl. "What would you like to eat?"

Norbu ate a good dinner and drank some tea. Then, turning his back, he made himself hiccup up a small piece of gold, which he gave to the girl's mother. Then he said to her, "Mother, I am feeling upset about some things that happened today. I would like to forget about them for awhile. Do you have any barley wine?"

"Yes, we have," the mother replied, "but it is not cheap. Do you have enough money for that, too?"

"I have plenty," said Norbu. "Bring me the barley wine now."

Norbu drank one cup of wine, then another, and then another. And because he wasn't used to drinking wine, he quickly became drunk. Soon he began to feel sick and dizzy, and he sat down in a corner to rest. In a few more minutes he was sound asleep. Then, because he was so drunk, he began to vomit in his sleep. The daughter came running when she heard the noise because she was afraid she would have to clean up a terrible mess. She was amazed to see that whenever Norbu vomited, a stream of gold came out of his mouth; he was surrounded by a pool of gold dust and lumps of gold.

"Mother, look at this!" the girl cried, running to get her mother. The mother came back to the room to see what was happening, and she and her daughter swept up all the gold that was lying on the floor around Norbu and put it in a leather bag. Just as they finished doing so, Norbu vomited again, so hard that the snake in his stomach came flying out of his mouth. Then he didn't vomit anymore.

"I know what this means," said the mother. "This is a *naga,* not a snake, and it is responsible for turning all of his spittle and vomit to gold. I will wash it off, and you must swallow it, my dear." So she washed the snake off and gave it to her daughter to swallow. She didn't want to do it, but finally she managed to get it down her throat. "Now give us some gold, my dear," said the mother. The girl spat in her hand, but she only got a handful of saliva; there was no gold there at all. Then the mother remembered that it was necessary to hiccup to make the gold appear; she hit her daughter between the shoulder blades to make her hiccup, and sure enough, a small lump of gold came out of her mouth. The girl and her mother were delighted to have what seemed to be a source of endless wealth.

The next morning, Norbu woke up with a terrible hangover. After having some tea he felt better and thought that it was time to leave. Wishing to thank his hostesses properly for taking care of him, he turned his back and hiccupped to get some more gold to give them. But nothing happened. He tried again, but still nothing happened. Thinking back to the night before, he had a dim memory of vomiting in his sleep and of the snake flying out of his mouth.

"Thieves!" he shouted. "What have you done with my snake? I demand you give it back to me."

"Snake?" said the mother. "What snake? What are you talking about?"

"You have stolen the gold-producing snake from my stomach," said Norbu. "I know you have."

"A snake in your stomach? What crazy talk is that? You must be a madman. Get out of my house at once. Go, go, get out." And the mother and the daughter picked up sticks and beat Norbu with them and drove him out of the house.

Now Norbu really couldn't go back home to his own country. Not only had he lost the king, but he had also lost his only source of wealth. Feeling very sad and discouraged, he started to walk toward a mountain pass in the distance.

As he reached the top of the pass, he heard the sounds of arguing and fighting and saw three boys fighting one another very bitterly. "Here, here, what's going on?" said Norbu. "Why are you fighting? You shouldn't be doing that." And he made the boys stop fighting and stand a little bit apart from one another.

"We're fighting over these things here," said what looked like the oldest boy. "A container, a pair of shoes, and a hat. We all want them, and we can't figure out how to divide them up."

"That sounds really foolish," said Norbu. "Who would fight over such common things? Surely you can find some way of dividing them up without fighting."

"They are not as common as they look," replied the boy. "The container is a magic food box. Whenever you want some *momo* dumplings, you just ask the box for them, open it up, and it is overflowing with *momo*. Or if you want cake, it will give you all the cake you can eat. It will give you any kind of food at all.

"The shoes are magic shoes. If you put them on, they will take you anywhere you want to go. And the hat is a magic hat. If you put it on, it will make you invisible. That's why we were fighting over these things."

"Yes, but there's a better way than that," said Norbu. "Why don't you have a race instead? Stand over there," he said, pointing to a big rock in the distance, "and when I raise my arm, you should all come running toward me. The first one here will get the container, the one who comes in second will get the shoes, and the one who comes last will get the hat. Do you all agree to that?"

The boys agreed and went over by the big rock to start the race. Immediately, Norbu picked up the container and the shoes and put on the hat. Suddenly he was invisible. Leaving the boys looking puzzled and angry, he walked away, laughing to himself.

He walked for some distance to make sure that the boys would not be able to find him again and then stopped to rest under a tree. As he was resting, a very big, ugly, dangerous-looking *sinpo* shape-shifter came out from behind the tree and began to walk toward him. Norbu was very afraid, but the shape-shifter didn't see him at all. Instead, he bent down and picked a blue flower; then he waved the flower in a circle three times in front of his face. Immediately the shape-shifter turned into a monkey, which climbed the tree and ate its fill of the fruit growing there. After awhile, it climbed down again, bent over, and picked a yellow flower. Waving this three times in front of its face, it turned into a *sinpo* again. "Hmm, this is very interesting," thought Norbu to himself.

After the shape-shifter had gone away, Norbu had some lunch from the magic food container. After that he bent down and picked one blue flower and one yellow flower. Then he stuffed the hat and the container into his shoulder-bag, put on the magic shoes, and said, "Take me to the front door of the house where I stayed last night." Immediately the shoes took him there, and when he arrived he quickly put on his hat to become invisible again. Looking at the house, he saw the daughter leaning out of the window. Taking the blue flower out of his bag, he waved it in a circle three times in front of her face, and she suddenly turned into an ugly, nasty-looking monkey and climbed up onto the roof of the house.

After awhile, the mother wondered where her daughter had gone and called out, "Daughter, come here. I need you to help me." So the monkey climbed down from the roof and went into the room where the mother was standing. "Oh, a monkey!" shouted the mother. "How nasty. How dreadful. What are you doing in the house? Get out, get out," she shouted, grabbing a broom and pushing the monkey toward the door.

"No, Mother, it's me, your daughter," the monkey said, desperately.

"What do you mean? My daughter is a beautiful girl, not an ugly monkey," said the mother. "What have you done with my daughter?"

"I'm afraid this is your daughter," said Norbu, taking off his hat and becoming visible again. "But she doesn't look so beautiful now. And I think she has a snake in her stomach."

"You terrible man," screamed the mother. "Bring my daughter back. Why are you always causing trouble for us?"

"I suppose I could bring her back," said Norbu, "but I want my snake back again. You must promise that as soon as I make the monkey into your daughter again, you will make her give the snake back to me. If you try to play any tricks, I will turn her into a monkey again, and next time, it will be permanent."

The mother of course had no choice but to agree, and so she begged Norbu to turn the monkey into her daughter again and promised to give the snake back right away. So Norbu waved the yellow flower in a circle three times in front of the monkey's face, and she became a beautiful young girl again. And right away, her mother made her drink some vinegar so she vomited up the snake.

"Thank you," said Norbu, swallowing the snake again. "I'll

be going now." And he turned away and hiccupped up a small lump of gold to give to the mother to show that he felt no resentment against her.

Then Norbu said to his shoes, "Take me to the palace of the kingdom where my friend has become the new king." Right away he arrived there and asked to see the king. When the king saw Norbu standing there, he was very happy and invited Norbu to come in to the palace for a feast and asked him to stay there for awhile.

"Thank you very much," said Norbu, "but I'd rather be getting back home. You should come home, too, you know."

"I'm sorry to say so, Norbu, but this new kingdom is much better than our old one. I'm very happy being king here, and I don't want to leave. But how about this: I'll issue a royal proclamation making you the king of the old kingdom in my place."

Norbu agreed to that, so soon he went home and the royal proclamation was read, making him king. The people were very happy because they remembered what a hero he was for volunteering to save the life of the prince many years before. And Norbu and his friend, the king, remained close friends, visiting each other's kingdom often, and the kingdoms were allies. The two kings lived for a long time, and their kingdoms grew strong and prosperous together.

BEFORE HE COULD THINK TWICE, Dersang said, "So Norbu got everything he wanted!" And Ngudup Dorjee came flying out of the broken bag again, giving Dersang a slap as he rushed back to the old cemetery.

The Shape-Shifter's Son

Once upon a time, in a certain small kingdom in a valley surrounded by high mountains, there was a king who loved very much to hunt and to eat meat. Hunting was his passion, and meat was his favorite food.

One day, the king was out hunting with his ministers when he saw a deer and immediately began to chase it. Soon the king was out of sight in the deep forest, and the ministers did not know where he had gone. The king, meanwhile, had lost sight of the deer and was in such a deep and dark part of the forest that he lost his way, even though he had hunted in that forest for his whole life. As he was standing beneath a tree trying to get his bearings, a *sinpo* shape-shifter came out from behind the tree, seized the king in a powerful grip, and carried him off to a cave.

It happened that this was a female shape-shifter, and although her face was not as ugly as that of most *sinpo,* she was still very ugly and hairy, with long pendulous breasts and sharp-pointed teeth. At first the king was sure that the shape-shifter would kill him and eat him right away, but to his surprise she simply kept him in the cave, feeding him and taking care of him and making sure that he did not escape. After several months, the shape-shifter made it clear that she wanted the king to have sex with her, and although he did not find her at all attractive, he was

also afraid of her so he complied with her wishes and became her lover. After a short while she became pregnant, and then she seemed to lose interest in the king. She stopped paying attention to him, and soon he was able to escape and make his way back to his palace.

The king's ministers had long since given him up for dead, and so they were overjoyed to see him walk out of the forest that day, safe and sound. Privately he told his ministers the story of being captured by the shape-shifter, but he didn't mention anything about the sex.

About ten months later, the people of the kingdom's capital city were very surprised to see a tall, hairy, very ugly woman walking down the main street carrying a baby in a blanket tied to her back. She didn't look either to the left or the right, but walked straight up to the palace gate. There she untied the blanket on her back, took out the baby, placed it in front of the palace gate, and walked away.

Later that day, the ministers gathered in the throne room, and the prime minister said, "I am very sorry to ask this, Your Majesty, but is there something else that you should have told us about the time you stayed with the shape-shifter?" The king, having little choice in the matter, acknowledged that the baby was undoubtedly the product of the time when he had sex with the female shape-shifter, and he would publicly acknowledge the child as his own. He named the baby Prince Dragpa.

Fortunately, Dragpa did not resemble his mother. In fact, he was a beautiful and intelligent-looking baby, with bright eyes and clear skin, and he had a cheerful disposition to match his good looks. The only resemblance to his mother was that his feet were big and hairy, like the feet of a gorilla, and the hair on top of his feet was striped like the stripes of a zebra. Behind his back, some people in the palace called him Stripe-foot. But really, not many people teased him or talked unkindly about him because he grew up to be a cheerful and friendly child, and almost everyone liked him.

As he grew older, Prince Dragpa also proved to be very intelligent, and his father relied very much on his advice. His father also married him to two beautiful princesses from neighboring kingdoms, and his life seemed to be very happy. Also as Dragpa grew older, one part of his ancestry became stronger because, even more than his father, he loved to hunt and loved to eat meat. He hardly would touch vegetarian food at all and insisted on eating meat every day.

After some years, the old king died, and the shape-shifter's son became king in his turn. The people of the kingdom were happy because Dragpa had been a very good prince. As king, he also showed that he would continue his father's wisdom and benevolence.

There happened to be, in the midst of a deep forest in that kingdom, an old hermit. And not just a hermit, but a very powerful holy man. People called him the Truth-Sayer Hermit because he had perfected his nature through seventeen reincarnations so that now every word he spoke was full of power, and anything that he predicted would come true. The old king had been the patron and protector of the Truth-Sayer Hermit, and the hermit came out of the forest every day at lunchtime to eat a specially prepared vegetarian meal that the king ordered for him from the palace kitchen. King Dragpa continued this custom so that even though neither father nor son liked to eat vegetarian food, there was always a proper vegetarian meal available for the hermit every day.

One day, not long after he had come to the throne, King Dragpa called his two wives to come to his chamber, and he said to them, "My father married me to both of you because he thought that was the proper thing to do. And it is true that I love you both, and also that you have both been good and respectful wives, and also that you have been very careful to get along with each other and not let any jealousy arise. Nevertheless, I think that it is bad policy in a kingdom for the king to have more than one wife, and so I have decided to send one of you away. The problem is that I love you both, and I haven't been able to decide which one of you I should divorce. Now I think I have the answer. Tomorrow, the two of you will have a horse race. You will start at the edge of the big forest, and when the starting flag is raised, you will race back here to the palace. Whichever one of you gets here first will continue to be my wife."

The next day, everything was done as the king had ordered. The two queens, mounted on fine horses, rode to the edge of the forest and waited for the starting flag. When it was raised, they began racing furiously back toward the palace.

Now it happened that one of the queens was very religious, while the other did not care very much about religion. As they were racing on the road back to the capital city, they passed a stupa, and the religious queen said to herself, "I have never passed this stupa before without making a circumambulation and offering prayers. It surely would be unsuitable for me to just ride past it now." So the queen turned her horse aside and made a circumambulation of the stupa. The other queen continued riding, and of course she arrived at the palace gate far in advance of the pious queen.

When the second queen reached the palace, she said to King Dragpa, "Your Majesty, it is quite clear that I lost the race, so I can no longer be your wife. I just would beg one favor from you, and that is for you to allow me to continue to be a queen for seven more days before you send me away."

King Dragpa was by no means a cruel man, and so of course

he agreed to grant the queen her request. The next day, still as queen, she ordered many workmen from the palace to take shovels and adzes, hammers and crowbars, and to follow her out along the road to the forest. When they reached the stupa the queen stopped and, raising her voice, she said, "Stupa! For many years I have honored you. I have always made circumambulations and offered prayers here, and I have always showed you respect. But now, instead of helping me, you hindered me so that I can no longer be queen. For that I am going to destroy you." And she ordered the workmen to destroy the stupa completely and level it down to the ground.

As they were working, the laborers raised a great cloud of dust; and some of them saw a shadowy figure fly up through the dust to the sky, where it disappeared.

After that the pious queen went away, and no one heard anything more about her again.

Not long after that, the Truth-Sayer Hermit happened to feel unwell, and he decided not to make the trip from the forest to the palace for his daily meal. And that was the moment that the dispossessed spirit of the destroyed stupa had been waiting for. Making his appearance and the sound of his voice exactly like that of the Truth-Sayer Hermit, he walked to the palace and came to the kitchen. But when his bowl of vegetarian food was sent out to him, he sent it back to the kitchen saying in an angry voice, "No more vegetarian food for me. I have renounced that diet completely. Send me meat! And not just your Buddhist vegetables disguised as meat, but real meat, a whole bowlful. And don't bother to cook it very much; I want to taste the flavor of flesh. From now on, that is what you must feed me." They brought him a bowl of half-cooked meat, which he devoured eagerly before going away.

The next day, the real Truth-Sayer Hermit returned to the palace. The unsuspecting royal cook brought out a bowl of meat for him. Thinking that it was made of vegetables prepared to look like meat, the hermit began to eat. But at the very first bite he spat the food out and shouted, "Meat! How dare you give me meat! For my entire life, I have never eaten meat, and now you have caused me to break my vows. What idiot has served me meat?"

"But, Your Honor," said the cook, "just yesterday you were here and told us to serve meat to you from now on."

"I? Here yesterday? Impossible," said the hermit. "Yesterday I felt unwell, and I did not leave the forest. How can you tell me that I was here yesterday?"

"But, sir, you were here," said the cook. "We all saw you and heard you."

"This is outrageous," said the hermit. "You are just telling more and more lies to cover up your incompetence. I won't stand for it. Here's what I say: If you all love meat so much, the time will come when King Dragpa eats nothing but human flesh for twelve long years." And with that he turned and walked back to the forest, and he never returned to the palace again.

The king was worried about the Truth-Sayer Hermit's curse that he would eat human flesh because everyone knew that the hermit's predictions always came true. But for a long time nothing happened, and so he began to forget about the unpleasant prophesy.

After several years, however, there came a day when the royal cook went to the market and found no meat to be had at all. The butchers had already sold all of their meat, all of the hunters had sold the last of their wild game, and there was no more meat anywhere. This was a disaster for the cook because the king would not eat anything but meat, and if there was no meat to serve to him he would surely become very angry. The cook sat down on a stone off to the side of the market to try to think about what to do. Then suddenly he heard a sound like many people weeping, and having nothing else to do, he went to see what was happening. He followed the sound to a certain house, and after he listened for awhile he understood that the family of that house was weeping because one of their children had just died. All of the family members had just come back from the cemetery.

As much as the idea filled him with horror, the cook knew that this was the answer to his problem. So he waited and listened some more until he understood from the people's conversation exactly where the child was buried. Then he went to the cemetery, waited until dark, dug up the child's body, wrapped it in a blanket, and carried it back to the palace. When he got there, he made sure that no one was watching, and he quickly cut up the body in small pieces and cooked it for the king's dinner.

After King Dragpa had eaten, he called the cook and said, "That was a really excellent dinner. What kind of meat was that?"

The cook hardly knew what to say, so he just replied, "Oh, Your Majesty, it was nothing special—just some ordinary kind of meat."

"What do you mean by giving me such an evasive answer?" said the king. "It must have been some particular kind of meat or other. Why won't you tell me what it was?"

"I'm sorry, Your Majesty, but there is a kind of special circumstance here. I'm afraid that if I told you what kind of meat that was, you would become very angry."

"I promise you that I will not."

"Even so, I don't want to tell you."

"Cook, it doesn't matter what you want. I command you to tell me right now."

Then the cook, trembling with fear, went very close to where King Dragpa was sitting and said, "I'm sorry, Your Majesty, but that was the flesh of a human child."

The king looked very thoughtful. "So, the curse is starting at last," he said to himself, "and there is nothing I can do now to evade it." To the cook, the king said, "That doesn't make me angry at all. In fact, it was so delicious that I insist that you serve it to me every night from now on."

The cook was horror-stricken. "But, Your Majesty," he said, "how can I do that? I happened to be able to find a dead child, but children don't die every day. How can I serve you the flesh of a child every day if none has died?"

"You've heard my commandment, Cook," said King Dragpa. "I'm sure you will do whatever you have to do to fulfill my orders."

So after that, the miserable cook spent every day listening for news that a child had died so he could sneak into a cemetery and rob the body from the grave. And on days when no child died naturally, he prowled the streets until he found an unguarded child to kill and cut up for the king's dinner. He tried to do this in different parts of the city to keep people from being suspicious, but very soon people began talking about how many children had disappeared and wondering what was happening to bring that horror to their kingdom. People began keeping their children at home and keeping a careful watch on them; this made the cook's job even more difficult, but still the children continued to disappear.

A group of men in one neighborhood decided to find out what was happening and put a stop to it. So they set a trap for the kidnapper by letting a young child play in the middle of a street where it seemed that no one was watching her. Then the men hid in the houses along the street to see what would happen.

Soon the cook came along, and he could hardly believe his good luck in finding a child that was so easy to steal. He had just laid his hands on her when all of the men jumped out from where they were hiding and began to give the cook a terrible beating. "Who are you? Why are you stealing our children?" they shouted at him.

"Wait, I recognize him," said one of the men. "He is the royal cook. Keep beating him until he tells us what's going on."

"No, I can't tell," said the cook. "The king will kill me."

"We will kill you right here and now if you don't tell us," said the men. So the cook, afraid for his life, told the men the whole story of how King Dragpa had begun eating the flesh of human children every day. When he had finished telling them, the men beat him some more until they finally left him lying in the street, bloody and broken.

Quickly the word spread through the whole city until soon there was a great crowd of men in front of the palace gates, armed with weapons and torches. "The king must come out," they shouted. "Come out now, king, or we will drag you out," they said.

The king realized that the mob would burn down his palace if he did not come out, so he walked out of the palace to where all the people were gathered at the gates. He tried to explain to them that it was not his fault that he had eaten their children because he had been put under a powerful curse, but of course no one would listen to him. Instead they grabbed him and began to beat him severely; then they picked him up and carried him to the execution ground.

"Please don't kill me. Have mercy, I beg you," King Dragpa pleaded.

"You showed no mercy to our children," the men said. "Black snow will fall from the sky before we let you go. Prepare for death because we are going to kill you now."

"Then I beg one thing of you. Let me pray before you kill me."

In that pious Buddhist kingdom, no one could refuse that request. So the men drew back a little way and formed a circle around the king and watched while he prayed.

Speaking very softly, the king prayed, "If I have accumulated any merit from all the years that I fed the Truth-Sayer Hermit, hear my prayer now. Give me wings to fly from this place and save my life."

King Dragpa indeed had accumulated merit from feeding the hermit for so many years, and suddenly a great pair of wings sprouted from his back. Spreading his wings, he flew up into the sky before the crowd knew what was happening. And then, as he flew, he was transformed into a kind of eagle-demon, with sharp talons and a long cruel beak. He swooped down over and over again at the crowd, tearing people's flesh with his talons and cutting them with his beak; finally he picked up one man and carried him off to a high rocky cliff to feast on his flesh.

After that the king remained an eagle-demon, and often he would fly down to catch another man and carry him to his nest high up on the cliff. After he had been doing this for quite some time, he won the great respect and admiration of all of the *sinpo* shape-shifters who lived in that part of the world because his demon shape was so powerful and he was so fierce and relentless in catching human victims to eat. Soon the shape-shifters decided that they would make him king of the *sinpo*.

"But in order to make you king," they said, "we must have a big banquet and a big party, with lots to eat. And not just ordinary humans, but only princes; only princes are good enough for a party like that. Please go to all of the small kingdoms in these mountains and valleys and begin to capture princes. When you have accumulated one thousand of them, we will have the banquet and crown you as our king."

There were many small kingdoms and many, many princes in that part of the world, so it was easy for the eagle-demon king to find them, but still it took a long time to capture so many of them. When he finally had nine hundred and ninety-nine princes locked up in a big compound, waiting for the banquet to begin, the shape-shifters said to the eagle-demon king, "It really would be best if you would capture Prince Suwasiti as the one-thousandth captive prince. He is the best and bravest prince in this whole part of the world, and he would make a perfect main course for our banquet."

The eagle-demon king agreed, so he flew to the kingdom of Prince Suwasiti's father and waited for a chance to capture the prince. After some days, he saw a good opportunity, so he swooped down, grabbed the prince in his fierce talons, and flew with him back to the prison compound. To everyone's surprise, Prince Suwasiti began to weep and tear his hair; bitter tears rolled down his cheeks, and nothing that anyone said would make him stop crying. The eagle-demon king came in and looked at him with contempt saying, "So this is the famous Prince Suwasiti, crying far more than any of these lesser princes did. Are you really so afraid of losing your life that you have lost all of your dignity first?"

"I am not at all afraid of dying," replied the prince, "for death comes to everyone sooner or later and is not to be feared. I am crying, instead, because in capturing me you have made me break my word, and my honor is precious to me. You have caused my honor to fail, and that is why I am weeping."

"How could I cause your honor to fail?" asked the eagle-demon king.

"Today, as I was going from the palace to the royal hunting park, I passed a Brahmin begging by the side of the road. He asked me for alms, and I replied that I had nothing to give him at that moment but if he would wait for me, I would surely give him something on my way back to the palace. Now that Brahmin will wait for a long time, and I will never be able to keep my promise. My honor is ruined," he said. And he began weeping again.

"Your Majesty, Eagle-King," said Prince Suwasiti, "would

you permit me now to return to my kingdom to give some alms to that Brahmin? I promise that I will come straight back here immediately when I have fulfilled my promise."

The eagle-demon king was impressed by Prince Suwasiti's sincerity, and so he agreed to let him go, though privately he didn't believe that he would voluntarily come back to the prison again. He began making plans to capture him again soon so the banquet could begin.

The eagle-demon king was very surprised, therefore, to see Prince Suwasiti walk into the prison compound the next day with a serene and confident look on his face. "I'm surprised to see you back," said the king. "Did you accomplish your aim of giving alms to the Brahmin?"

"Yes, I did," replied the prince, "and the Brahmin in turn gave me a teaching that will give me strength as I face the ordeal of being eaten by you and the other shape-shifters. He said:

The end of birth is death;
The end of construction is destruction;
The end of accumulation is dispersal;
The end of meeting is parting."

Just as the prince said those words, the exact moment arrived of the end of King Dragpa's twelve years as an eater of human flesh. He felt a great burden lift from his soul, and he resumed his old human shape again, striped hairy feet and all. Ignoring the protests of the shape-shifters, the king opened the doors of the prison compound and let all of the captive princes go free.

"But I'm afraid that I can never return to my old kingdom," he said to Prince Suwasiti. "The people will never forgive me for killing and eating their children."

"Let me go with you and try to reason with them," said the

prince. "I will explain to them that the fault did not lie with you, but rather with the Truth-Sayer Hermit who put a terrible curse on you for no reason. He was very badly mistaken, and the consequences of that all fell on you. I think they will understand."

So they traveled together to King Dragpa's old country, and Prince Suwasiti spoke to the assembled people with great eloquence and reason. Soon all of the people were persuaded, and they forgave the king. Then he resumed being their king, and he ruled over that kingdom peacefully and happily for many years.

The King Stands Up

Once there was a king of a wealthy and powerful country who worried that people might try to take advantage of him. He realized that he himself was too honest and trusting to see through all of the ingenious schemes that people might have to try to get money from the royal purse, so he decided to appoint the cleverest person he could find to be his advisor. "If I have a really smart chief minister, my treasury will be safe," he thought. He decided that the best way to see who the cleverest person in his whole kingdom was would be to hold a contest.

Soon messengers went out in all directions, and they put up notices in the main market square of every town and village in the kingdom. "All clever talkers are ordered to report to the palace on such-and-such a day to take part in a royal challenge."

On the appointed day, the royal audience hall was full of people, all of whom considered themselves to be extremely clever. They were chatting among themselves, trying to figure out what this royal challenge might be. Their talking died down suddenly when the king entered the hall, and they soon found out what was expected of them.

"Gentlemen," said the king, "I believe that you are certainly the cleverest people in my kingdom. I want to find out which of you is the cleverest of all, and so I make a challenge to you. I am

going to sit down on my throne now, and I do not intend to stand up again while any of you are still in this room. But if anyone can persuade me to stand up from my throne, I will make him the chief minister of the kingdom."

Well, the contestants tried, one after another, to make the king stand up, and they all failed. One clapped his hands loudly, trying to startle the king into jumping from his seat, but the king was not fooled by that. Another tried to persuade the king that the palace was on fire and that he should get up and run out of the palace to save his life, but the king just laughed at him. Some used elaborate arguments from classical philosophy to demonstrate why it was morally and mathematically necessary for the king to stand up, but the king just found them boring. One after the other, each clever talker failed, and the room became more and more empty as the unsuccessful contestants left to go back to their villages empty-handed.

Finally a young boy named Yeshi, hardly out of middle school but already a good talker and very grown-up for his age, stood in front of the throne.

"Really, Your Majesty," Yeshi said, "this business of making you stand up from your throne is so trivial that I think it is not worthy of my talents. I beg permission to try a much more difficult feat."

"Oh?" said the king. "What would that be?"

"Do you think, Your Majesty," answered Yeshi, "that anyone could make you go through a door against your will?"

"I'm sure nobody could do that," said the king. "Why would I go through a door if I didn't want to?"

"And yet I believe I could do so," said Yeshi, pointing to the door of the throne room. "Suppose you were standing outside that door. What would you give me if I were able to make you step over the doorsill and come back into the throne room, try as you might to resist it?"

"If you can do that," said the king, "I will give you half of all of my wealth, in addition to making you the chief minister of the kingdom."

"Very well," said Yeshi. "Shall we begin?"

And the king stood up and began to walk toward the door.

Penba and Dawa

Penba and Dawa were very good friends. Dawa was a weaver, and so was his wife. They made their living by weaving and selling cloth, and although they were far from rich, they were comfortable enough. Penba was a magician who entertained people in the marketplace or at festivals and parties in the homes of rich people.

Sometimes Dawa teased Penba about his profession. "Do you really think that being a magician is an honest way to make a living? All you do is fool people with tricks that aren't real magic."

"Oh, what do you know about it?" Penba would reply.

But teasing and joking couldn't spoil their friendship, and they relied on each other as friends should do.

One day, as Dawa and his wife were having lunch, they heard a knock on the door. Leaving his half-eaten food on his plate, Dawa went to the door and found Penba standing there with a horse.

"Dawa, I'd like your help," said Penba. "I'm thinking of buying this horse, but I don't know very much about horses. I don't know if this one is too young or too old, or if it will be a good horse for me to ride. Would you take a look at it for me?"

"I'd be glad to," said Dawa, and he walked all around the

horse, looking at it closely. He looked into its mouth and under its tail, lifted up its hooves, and ran his hands along its back. "It looks alright," said Dawa, "but I'd like to ride it before I advise you to buy it, just to make sure."

Dawa mounted the horse and started to ride on the main road out of town. After awhile he was satisfied with the horse and wanted to get back to his lunch, so he pulled on the reins and said, "Whoa." The horse just kept going. Dawa pulled harder on the reins and said "whoa" in a louder voice, but the horse just began running faster. The harder Dawa pulled on the reins and the more he said "whoa," the faster the horse ran, until Dawa was putting all of his attention into just hanging on. The horse ran like that without stopping for five days, following whatever roads it wanted to, until finally it came to a halt at the edge of the sea.

"This is a long way from Tibet," thought Dawa. "I never thought I would see the ocean in this lifetime. I'll just get down and see what the water feels like." So Dawa dismounted and reached for the reins to lead the horse down to the water. But as soon as Dawa got off the horse, the horse began running again, just as fast as before, and soon it was out of sight across a mountain pass.

"This is terrible," thought Dawa. "Here I am hundreds of miles from home, and I have no idea which roads to take to get back again even if I could walk that far. What should I do?"

Then, with nothing else to do, he began walking along the beach. Soon he saw on a hillside overlooking the water a small house. So he walked up and knocked on the door. An old woman came to the door, and he explained to her that he had come from another country and his horse had run away. Could he please have something to eat and drink, and could he stay the night? The old woman's husband had been listening also while Dawa told his story, and after the old couple had talked it over, they agreed that Dawa could be their guest.

That evening, as they were sitting down to supper, a beautiful young woman came into the room. "This is our daughter, Yangchen," the old woman said. Dawa was immediately struck by the daughter's beauty and her pleasant manner, and he soon felt that he was falling in love with her, forgetting all about his wife back home. Yangchen also found Dawa very handsome and appealing, and soon she began to fall in love with him also.

After supper, the old man said to Dawa, "For a long time, we have worried that our daughter has not found a husband yet. If you agree, you and she could get married, and you could continue to live here with us."

Not thinking at all about his wife back home, Dawa agreed to that suggestion. He and Yangchen were married soon afterward, and they had a very happy and loving life together. After nine months, Yangchen had a baby boy, and in the next few years they had two more children. All three of the children were bright and cheerful, and their parents were very proud of them. The only sad thing that happened during these years was that Yangchen's elderly parents died.

One beautiful, sunny day, Yangchen suggested that the whole family go for a picnic on the beach. This seemed like a fine idea, so they took baskets of food and jugs of water down to the seashore and began to relax near the water. "Don't go in the deep water," they called to the children. But just then a huge wave came onto the shore and swept the youngest child out to sea. The middle child dove into the water to try to save his younger sister, but he too got caught in the huge wave and was swept away. Immediately the oldest son rushed into the water to try to save his brother and sister, but he also disappeared and was drowned.

Yangchen and Dawa were stunned by what had happened. In hardly more than a minute they had lost their whole family. Still in a state of shock, Yangchen ran to the ocean, flung herself into the waves, and was drowned. Dawa was left standing on the beach, completely alone.

As he was standing there, the same horse that had brought him there years before came trotting up and stood quietly as Dawa mounted him and settled into the saddle. There was no reason for Dawa to stay in a place that had brought him so much sadness, so he wanted to go away at once.

As before, the horse began to run straight ahead and would not let Dawa stop him or guide him at all. But after awhile the roads began to look familiar to Dawa, and he realized that the horse was taking him back to his old home. Then he began to wonder: "Will my old wife recognize me? Will she be glad to have me back? Will she be an old woman by now? How about Penba, will he still be my friend?"

Dawa felt quite agitated by the time the horse stopped in front of his door. He rushed into his house and found himself kneeling by his wife's side with tears pouring down his cheeks. "My darling wife, I'm so sorry," he blurted out. "I've been gone so many years. You must have been terribly worried about me. But not only that, but I married another woman and had children with her. You must think I'm a terrible person. Can you ever forgive me? The whole problem was that the horse wouldn't stop. . . ."

"What are you talking about?" said the wife, with an alarmed look on her face. "Horse? Another wife? Been away for years? Have you lost your mind? You've just been sitting here for the past few minutes with a faraway look on your face, and you wouldn't respond to anything I said. I hope you're not going crazy. Here, my love," she said, pushing the half-full plate of food in front of him, "why don't you finish your lunch? I'm sure you'll feel better after that."

The Dream Eater

"Dersang," said Lord Nagarjuna, "you will have to try again. Just remember how tricky Ngudup Dorjee is. He will always try to tell you stories, and I understand how hard it is for you not to listen. Just be very careful not to say anything at all until you have brought him all the way back here to the cave."

"Don't worry, Lord Nagarjuna," said Dersang. "I've learned my lesson now. I'm sure I'll be able to bring him back this time without saying anything at all."

"We'll see," said Nagarjuna, "but I hope you're right. Anyway, here's another container of special food, a new sack and strap, and the trusty old axe. Off you go, now."

This time the walk to the old cemetery didn't seem so long because it was already becoming familiar, and Dersang didn't have too much trouble finding where the path through the cemetery wall had shifted to this time. Once inside, he shouted, "Where is Ngudup Dorjee?" and ignoring the hundreds of spirits that all answered back "Here, here, over here, here I am," he immediately saw the real Ngudup Dorjee trying to get away unseen. Dersang followed him and soon saw him climbing a tall tree.

"Come down, Ngudup Dorjee, or I'll chop your tree down," said Dersang.

"Save your axe," said Ngudup Dorjee. "You've caught me again."

Ngudup Dorjee climbed down the tree, and Dersang immediately seized him by the neck and threw him into the sack. Pulling the leather strap tight, he hoisted the sack onto his shoulder and started on the long walk home.

"Well, boy, it seems we have some time on our hands," said Ngudup Dorjee, his voice slightly muffled from being inside the sack. "How about a story to make the walk a little easier? And don't be in too much of a hurry; this is a long story, and you wouldn't want to miss the ending."

Even though Dersang was very afraid of what might happen if Ngudup Dorjee told another story, of course he couldn't say anything to stop him. "I just have to remember not to say anything at all, no matter what happens," he thought to himself. And as soon as Ngudup Dorjee began to speak, Dersang found that he couldn't keep himself from listening.

ONCE UPON a time (said Ngudup Dorjee), there was a certain very small kingdom. And in that kingdom lived a boy who was called the Dream Eater. He had that rather strange name because of his unusual talent, which was that he had many, many dreams, and he always remembered them when he woke up. Not only that, but he could always understand what the dreams meant, and whenever he said that a dream contained some sort of prediction, the prediction always came true.

The Dream Eater lived alone with his old widowed mother, and when he was just a little boy she saw immediately that he had a very special power. She told the king about it and after making the boy tell him a few dreams and explain what they meant, the king quickly saw that everything the mother said was true. So he made the boy his royal dream interpreter, and his mother became his official guardian. They received a salary from the palace treasury that enabled them to live in comfort together. And the boy explained many dreams to the king and told him many accurate predictions, so with the boy's help the king was able to make his kingdom rich and strong and safe from its enemies. Sometimes, when the Dream Eater had told the king a dream that was particularly pleasing or helpful, the king would order that the boy be rewarded with gifts of gold or silk, and the boy grew very fond of expensive and beautiful things.

The mother took good care of her son, and the boy loved his mother very much. But sometimes, even so, they did not get along with each other and even quarreled once or twice because the mother felt that the Dream Eater was becoming arrogant about being one of the king's favorites and also because when the king gave him extra rewards he did not want to share them with his mother. So even though things were going well for them, the mother sometimes worried about her son.

One night, something strange happened. The mother woke up in the middle of the night because she heard her son laughing loudly in his room. Going to look at him, she saw that he was still sleeping, but laughing wildly in his sleep.

Waking him up, she said to him, "Son, son, you must be having a dream. Tell me what you are dreaming and what it means. This has never happened before so you must be having a very special and unusual dream."

It took the boy a minute or two to wake up completely, and then he said, "No, Mother, it's nothing special. It was just a funny dream that made me laugh. It doesn't have any meaning at all."

"No, no, that can't be true. It has to have some meaning. Why won't you tell me what it is? What is so special about this dream that you won't even tell it to your mother?"

"No, I'm telling you the truth. It was just a funny dream. Go away and let me go back to sleep."

"Yes, that's a good idea. Go back to sleep and finish your dream. Then maybe you will know what it means, and you can explain it to me in the morning. Surely this is something that we must tell the king about."

"Good night, Mother. I'm going back to sleep and you should, too," said the Dream Eater. "Believe me, this is nothing at all."

In the morning, when both mother and son were having their breakfast, the mother asked again about the dream.

"Really, Mother, it was just a funny dream, that's all. This is exactly what I saw. There was a road, and walking along the road was a large louse that had another louse riding on its back. They looked so funny that I laughed out loud. But I'm sure that it has no meaning; I don't feel anything like I usually feel when one of my dreams makes a prediction."

"I don't believe you. I think there must be something that you aren't telling me about this dream. If you don't tell me right away, I will report it to the king."

"Mother, you may do as you like. I have nothing more to say about this dream."

Later that morning the mother went to the royal palace and told the king that the Dream Eater had had an unusual dream that he didn't want to talk about. "He has no respect for his aged mother anymore," she said, "but perhaps he will explain the meaning of his dream to you."

The king immediately sent two court officers to the house where the Dream Eater lived with his mother and told him to report to the palace at once. When he was standing in the throne room, the king said to him, "Your mother tells me that you've had an unusual dream that you won't talk about. What's this all about?"

"Really, Your Majesty," said the Dream Eater, "I don't know why my mother is making such a fuss about this. It was just a funny dream with no meaning. There isn't anything more I can say about it."

Now this king was very kind and generous to people who did what he wanted them to, and when he was happy everyone around him was happy, too. But when a person did not obey one of the king's commands quickly enough, or when the king felt that someone was going against his will, he could be very angry and cruel. And the king became very angry at the Dream Eater when he heard those words.

"You dare to refuse me?" he thundered. "What secret meaning does this dream have that you are concealing from me? Guards! Seize this man," he commanded. "Throw him into the dungeon hole until he learns better manners."

The dungeon hole was a terrible place located in a far corner of the palace grounds. It was a deep underground hole cut out of solid rock, with high, steep sides and only a very small opening at the top. Usually when a person was put into the dungeon hole, he died of hunger and thirst after a very short time. The floor of the hole was covered with the bones of people who had died there, and the walls were crawling with horrible insects that waited to eat the flesh of any new prisoner who would soon become a corpse.

But the Dream Eater was a much tougher and more determined young man than anyone who had ever been put in the dungeon hole before. When he became thirsty, he drank water from the noxious puddles on the floor of the hole. When he became hungry, he caught the insects that clung to the walls of the hole and ate them alive, so that these insects that had grown fat from eating corpses now became food themselves. And, strange to say, the Dream Eater not only survived on this diet, but he grew taller and stronger and healthier than ever.

One day, as the Dream Eater was resting on the floor of the hole, he happened to look up and saw two crows perched on the rim of the opening of the hole, high above his head.

The female crow said to the male, "Husband, are there any human beings around that you can see? I have something to tell you but I don't want to be overheard."

The male crow looked around and said, "No, there are no humans around at all, except of course for this miserable person at the bottom of the hole. But you needn't bother about him. He probably can't hear what we are saying, and he will be dead soon anyway. You may speak freely, my love."

"Well, here's what I want to tell you," said the female crow. "Of course you know that human beings often have dreams, and sometimes the dreams are so remarkable that the humans want them to come true. But that very seldom happens; dreams are like wishes, and most of the time they do not become reality.

"Now the king of this country owns a magical lasso called the Sun Ray Lasso and a magical hook called the Moon Ray Hook. These things can be used to turn dreams into reality, but the king himself knows nothing about this so he doesn't suspect what marvelous treasures he owns. But just recently I was at the Marble Rock Pool on the other side of the mountain, and I learned how these magical tools can be used.

"Perhaps you have never been to the Marble Rock Pool, so I will describe it to you. There is a big rock of pure white marble, and it is surrounded on all sides by a large pool of crystal-clear water. On the fifteenth night of the lunar month, the night of the full moon, some strange things happen there. At midnight, six thousand beautiful girls come down from heaven to the pool, and they all bathe there, splashing themselves with water, showering in the cascades that come down from the marble rock, and washing their hair. When they have finished, they ascend up to heaven again.

"Then six thousand angels descend from heaven and bathe in the pool as well, showering in the cascades and washing their hair; and when they have finished they ascend back to heaven. Finally, six thousand *naga*-girls come down from heaven with the bodies of beautiful maidens and with dragon heads and serpent tails, and they too bathe in the pool. And when they have finished bathing and showering and washing their hair, thousands of flower petals fall from the sky like rain, floating on the surface of the water. And then all of the *naga*-girls ascend back to heaven—all, that is, except for one girl who stays behind to gather up some of the flower petals to take back to heaven with her. She is unusual-looking also because her dragon nose is very long and tied into a knot at the end, so she is easy to recognize. And if, at just the right moment, you capture her with the Sun Ray Lasso and seize her with the Moon Ray Hook, she will have to tell you how to make your dreams come true."

Of course, the Dream Eater listened very carefully to every word the female crow was saying, without moving or making a sound or doing anything to frighten the crows away. And after the crows had finished their conversation and flown off, he thought to himself, "That is how I will make my escape."

A few days later, the king's daughter, Princess Palmo, happened to be playing in the far corner of the palace where the dungeon hole was located. And as she and her friends were running around, she stopped and looked into the hole. She was quite surprised to see the Dream Eater down there.

"Princess," called the Dream Eater, "do you remember me? I remember you. I would be very grateful if you would take a message to your father for me. Tell him that now I might be able to interpret my strange dream for him."

"I'll tell him," said Princess Palmo, and she ran off to the palace.

"Father," she said, "Remember the Dream Eater that we threw into the dungeon hole a long time ago? I just now saw him still down at the bottom of the hole. Who would have thought he'd still be alive after all this time? And he even looks stronger and healthier than he did before. He is certainly a remarkable person. He asked me to tell you that now he thinks he can interpret that dream for you."

"It's about time," said the king. "If he weren't such a stubborn and difficult young man, he could have told me a long time ago. Anyway," he said, turning to his palace guards, "bring him to me and we'll see what he has to say."

"Actually, Your Majesty," said the Dream Eater when he had been brought to the royal audience hall, "I still don't know exactly what that dream means. But I do know now how to find out. I understand that you have a magic lasso called the Sun Ray Lasso and a magic hook called the Moon Ray Hook. If you will lend those to me, I will use them to find out the meaning of my strange dream."

The king was very suspicious of this request, but he was also still curious about the dream. So finally he ordered a servant to fetch the magic lasso and the magic hook and gave them to the Dream Eater. "Here they are," the king said. "Make sure you take good care of them, and bring them back soon."

The Dream Eater took the magic lasso and the magic hook, and as soon as he left the palace he traveled across the mountain to the Marble Rock Pool, where he waited for the full moon on the fifteenth night of the lunar month.

When the full moon night finally came, everything happened just as the female crow had described. The big white marble rock glistened in the moonlight, and it was surrounded on all sides by a large pool of crystal-clear water. Just at midnight, he saw six thousand beautiful girls descend from heaven to bathe in the pool, splashing themselves with water, showering in the cascades that came down from the marble rock, and washing their hair. When they had finished, they all went back up to heaven again.

Then six thousand angels descended from heaven. They bathed in the pool as well, and showered in the cascades and washed their hair; and when they finished, they all rose into the sky and went back to heaven. Finally, six thousand *naga*-girls came down from heaven, and they all had the bodies of beautiful maidens with dragon heads and serpent tails, and they too bathed in the pool. And when they had finished bathing and showering and washing their hair, thousands of flower petals fell from the sky like rain, floating on the surface of the water. Then all of the *naga*-girls ascended back to heaven, except for one girl, who stayed behind to gather up some of the flower petals. She was very unusual looking, with a long dragon nose tied into a knot near the end. And just as she was picking up a big armful of flower petals to take back to heaven with her, the Dream Eater threw the Sun Ray Lasso and captured her. Holding the Moon Ray Hook ready in case she tried to escape, the Dream Eater approached the girl.

"Oh!" screamed the girl. "Who are you and what are you doing?" Then she calmed down and said, "You don't even need to answer me. I know who you are, and I know everything about you. I've been expecting you to come here. Now you have caught me, and I must do whatever you wish me to do. But you must follow my instructions carefully if you want things to work out well. Let me tell you what is going to happen next.

"You must put your arms around my body, hold on very

tightly to me, and close your eyes. Then I will jump into the crystal pool while you are holding on to me. When we reach the bottom of the pool, I will tell you to open your eyes again, and you will see a beautiful palace. The palace will be covered with gold and silver, and turquoise and coral and lapis lazuli, and many other kinds of treasures; it will be a more beautiful palace than anything you have ever seen or imagined. Standing at the top of the staircase of the palace will be a beautiful maiden named Saledam. You must hide behind me and not let her see you; and then while I distract her by talking with her, you must find a way to get behind her, still remaining unseen.

"She will greet me and welcome me back to the palace and ask how I am. And I will say to her, 'I am well, sister, but I was at the Marble Rock Pool this evening, and I saw a human there. The sight of a human in that sacred place made me feel all dirty and impure, and so I am feeling a bit distressed.' Just as I say that, you must punch Saledam very hard in the back. She will cry out in pain and look behind her to see what caused it, but you must move very quickly so that she can't see you. She will say to me, 'Sister, what has caused me this pain? I have never felt anything so terrible in my life.' I will say to her, 'Oh, my dear sister, I'm afraid this must be my fault. I was at the Marble Rock Pool when it was being profaned by a human, and now I'm afraid that the pollution has spread from me to you and is causing you pain.'

"Then you must hit her again and again in the back, without mercy, so that she cries out in pain again. And again she will ask me the cause, and I will explain to her that the pollution I suffered at the Marble Rock Pool has spread to her and is causing pain to her body. Then I will suggest that she call her father, the Naga Lama, to see if he can help.

"She will agree to this, of course, and so her father will come quickly to the palace, riding on a tiger. While he is busy dismounting from the tiger, you will come out from behind Princess Saledam and stand in a very fierce pose with one leg raised and one arm raised and one eye closed, and you will wait for the Naga Lama to speak. 'Who are you, and what kind of demon are you?' he will ask. Then you must say, 'I am a fierce one-eyed demon from the upper regions, and you must give me whatever I want.' And Saledam, who by this time will have forgotten all about the pain in her body, will say, 'Yes, I've heard that there is just such a one-eyed demon in the upper regions, and he is very fierce.' 'What do you want, then?' the Naga Lama will ask you. And you must reply, 'I want your daughter, Saledam. She must belong to me.' Then the Naga Lama, who will be very afraid of you, will agree to give Saledam to you. 'When do you want her?' he will ask. 'Tomorrow morning,' you should reply. And that is how you will come to have Princess Saledam for yourself, and she will help you to make your dreams come true."

All of that sounded very good to the Dream Eater, so he held tightly to the body of the *naga*-girl with the long dragon nose with a knot in it and closed his eyes. She jumped into the crystal pool, and when she told him to open his eyes again, he saw a palace that was more beautiful than anything he had ever seen or imagined. It was covered with gold and silver, and turquoise and coral and lapis lazuli, and many other kinds of treasures; it was so beautiful it took his breath away. Standing at the top of the staircase of the palace was the most beautiful girl he had ever seen, and he knew that this must be Saledam. So just as he had been told to do, he hid behind the *naga*-girl so that Saledam couldn't see him; and then as Saledam and the *naga*-girl greeted each other, he ran very quickly to get behind Saledam before she noticed him.

Saledam welcomed the *naga*-girl back to the palace and asked her how she was. The *naga*-girl replied, "I am well, sister, but I was at the Marble Rock Pool this evening, and I saw a human there.

The sight of a human in that sacred place made me feel all dirty and impure, and so I am feeling a bit distressed." Just as she said that, although he really did not want to do it, the Dream Eater punched Saledam very hard in the back. She cried out in pain and looked behind her to see what caused it, but the Dream Eater moved very quickly so she couldn't see him.

Saledam said, "Sister, what has caused me this pain? I have never felt anything so terrible in my life."

The *naga*-girl replied, "Oh, my dear sister, I'm afraid this must be my fault. I was at the Marble Rock Pool when it was being profaned by a human, and now I'm afraid that the pollution has spread from me to you and is causing you pain."

Then the Dream Eater hit her again and again in the back, without mercy, so that she cried out in pain, even louder than before. And again she asked the *naga*-girl what was causing the pain, and she explained that the pollution she suffered at the Marble Rock Pool had spread to her and was causing her pain. Then she suggested to Saledam that she call her father, the Naga Lama, to see if he could help cure the pain.

Saledam quickly sent a servant to find the Naga Lama, who in a short while came to the palace, riding on a tiger. While he was busy dismounting from the tiger, the Dream Eater came out from behind Saledam and stood some distance away in a very fierce pose with one leg raised and one arm raised and one eye closed. As soon as the Naga Lama saw him, he shouted, "Who are you, and what kind of demon are you?"

The Dream Eater replied in a very loud voice, "I am a fierce one-eyed demon from the upper regions, and you must give me whatever I want."

Saledam, who by this time had forgotten all about the pain in her back, said, "Yes, I've heard that there is just such a one-eyed demon in the upper regions, and he is very fierce."

"What do you want, then?" the Naga Lama asked.

The Dream Eater replied, "I want your daughter, Saledam. She must belong to me."

Then the Naga Lama, who was very afraid of this terrible demon, agreed to give Saledam to him. "When do you want her?" he asked.

"Tomorrow morning," the Dream Eater replied.

"Come back then," said the Naga Lama, "and she will be ready for you."

The Dream Eater was shown to a room in the palace, where he went to sleep thinking of Princess Saledam. The next morning he awoke and went quickly to the audience room of the palace to claim his bride. But where there had been a beautiful palace of gold and silver and gemstones, there was now only a miserable group of stone and mud huts; and where Princess Saledam had been standing, a dirty brown dog lay sleeping in the dust. The Dream Eater could hardly believe his eyes, and he was furious about being tricked in this way. There seemed to be nothing else to do than to try to get away and find his way back home. "Come along, then," he said to the dog, and they began to walk away together.

They walked and walked until they reached the ocean shore. As the day wore on, the Dream Eater began to get very hungry and thirsty, and in his anger and frustration he picked up a stick and beat the dog with it. The dog ran away for a short distance, and then began to dig a hole in the ground. Soon she had uncovered some *ba* barley-and-butter balls, and both the man and the dog ate some of them; they tasted very delicious. The country they were walking through, near the seashore, seemed to be nothing but a desert of stones and dust. The Dream Eater became more and more thirsty, and more and more angry. Soon he beat the dog again; she ran for some distance and began to bark. When the Dream Eater looked to see what she was barking at, he saw that she had found a small spring, where they both drank some water. Later that evening, he beat the dog once more; she ran away, dug a hole in the ground, and found some roast mutton that they had for supper.

Things went on like that for a few days, and finally the dog looked up at the Dream Eater and said to him (to his great surprise, because he had no idea the dog could talk), "You don't know anything at all about dogs, do you? You think you have to beat me so I'll find food and water for you, but there are much better ways of getting food than that. Why don't you take your hunting dogs" (and here she looked to the side near where the Dream Eater was standing, and suddenly there was a pair of fine hunting dogs sitting right next to him) "and go catch some animals that we both can eat."

The next morning, the Dream Eater went off early with the hunting dogs, confident that he would be able to catch some deer or rabbits or perhaps at least a couple of marmots that they could eat for dinner. But to his disappointment, they didn't see any animals at all, and he returned to their camp empty-handed. But when he got back, he was astonished to find the dog sitting in front of a handsome stone house, with a kitchen shed off to the side and some food cooking on the stove. "How can this have happened?" he wondered. The dog looked glad to see him, but didn't say anything at all to explain how the house came to be there, so he went to bed feeling very puzzled.

The next day he again went hunting with his dogs, but was unable to catch anything. And again when he got back to the house he was surprised, because now the house was a big two-story mansion, with nicely carved wooden doors and windows and a handsome garden. "How did this happen?" he wondered, but the dog did not explain anything to him about what was going on.

On the third day, the Dream Eater said to the dog, "I don't

think I'll bother going hunting today. We never catch anything anyway."

But the dog replied, "No, it's better if you go hunting even if you come back empty-handed; you never know what you might find."

So the Dream Eater took his dogs and pretended to go off on a hunt. But really he only went a short distance away and hid behind some rocks to see what would happen.

To his surprise, the dog turned into the beautiful Princess Saledam, who directed a large workforce of *naga*s who were busy enlarging the mansion into a real palace, decorated with gold and silver and precious stones and fine carpets. So the Dream Eater went off with his hunting dogs, feeling very puzzled about what was happening. When he came back that evening, he saw that the fine palace was all finished, and he also saw in front of the palace a large box full of all kinds of animals that were talking with his dog. One frog was saying, "It's too bad this human is making so much trouble for us. It is very hard to help him when he will not follow your advice. But anyway we must try to help him as much as we can."

So the Dream Eater realized that these animals were the *naga*s that had been working on the palace and his dog was Princess Saledam in disguise. So he ran into the courtyard of the palace and immediately seized the dog, ripped off its skin, and threw it into the fire. "Well, master, now you will have me as Princess Saledam all the time because you have destroyed my disguise," said the *naga* princess. "I'm afraid, though, that this will create problems for us. Not big problems that we can't handle, but problems nevertheless. You'd better be very careful to take my advice about things from now on, or things will just get worse." And after that the Dream Eater and Saledam lived together in the palace as husband and wife.

One day, not long afterward, the Dream Eater was sitting at the window of his palace when, in the far distance, he saw a big flock of sheep on a mountainside. Looking more carefully, he saw that the shepherd was the shepherd of the king's flocks, someone who he had known well back in the days when he himself was the royal interpreter of dreams. He told Saledam what he had seen, and she said, "This could be trouble. Be mindful of what you say. You must be very careful not to tell him too much." Quickly she set to work with magic to remove all of the beauty from the palace and the gardens. The buildings were still there, but all of their beauty had been changed into beams of light, which she put into a strong wooden treasure box, closed the cover, and put away inside the house. The Dream Eater's clothes, which had been fine and handsome to match the palace, turned into ordinary ragged clothes, and Saledam herself was transformed into a short, ugly, deformed old woman. "Whatever you do, don't give away the secret!" she said to her husband.

Soon, the shepherd came up to the house and recognized his old friend the Dream Eater. "This is quite a big house that you have here, although I must say it is also rather ugly. Still, you seem to have done very well for yourself. Does all this belong to you?"

"No, no, it's not mine," said the Dream Eater. "The owner is not here right now. I'm only one of his servants." But as they talked more, the shepherd kept making comments about how ugly the house was, with doors that didn't fit the doorframes, and stones that were roughly cut, and everything out of proportion; and the Dream Eater felt that his pride was being insulted, and he became more and more angry. "So you think this is ugly, do you?" he shouted. "Well, you should see what it's really like." And he rushed into the house, brought out the treasure box, and opened the lid, whereupon all of the light flew out and became the beauty of the palace again; and the shepherd was dazzled by what he saw.

"Husband, that was a big mistake," said Saledam. "This is going to cause trouble for us. You really need to learn to be more mindful of what you are doing. You took away and burned my dog skin, so I can no longer disguise myself in order to help you. I will do what I can, but you have made things very difficult." And sure enough, no sooner had the shepherd left their palace than he ran to the king's palace and told the king everything that he had seen.

"I certainly need to see this for myself," said the king. "Besides, the Dream Eater never returned my Sun Ray Lasso and my Moon Ray Hook; this will give me a good chance to ask for them back."

The very next day, the king and some of his guards got on their horses and rode out to where the Dream Eater and Princess Saledam were living, guided by the shepherd. The Dream Eater saw them coming a very long way away and told Saledam. Once again she removed all the beauty from the palace, turned it into rays of light, and locked them up in the treasure box. "Whatever you do, don't open the box," she told her husband. "If you do, our troubles will only get worse."

When the king arrived, everything looked just as it had when the shepherd first saw it. The Dream Eater said that the owner of the big, ugly palace was away, and he insisted that he was only a servant and that the deformed old woman standing nearby was one of the housekeepers. "He's lying," whispered the shepherd to the king. "If you insult his pride, he will not be able to contain his anger, and he will reveal the true nature of this place to you." So the king teased the Dream Eater about how he had come down in the world, how he had once been an honored royal retainer but was now only a servant to the master of the ugliest palace in the world and was dressed in rags. "Oh, is that what you think?" shouted the Dream Eater. "Take a look at this, then." And he opened the treasure box, and immediately the beauty of the palace sparkled forth everywhere; he himself was dressed in splendid clothing and jewels. Worst of all, the king could clearly see that Saledam was the most beautiful woman that he or anyone else had ever seen.

"I must get this palace for myself," thought the king. "And what is more, I must get *her* for myself." Aloud, he said to the Dream Eater, "I am the king, but your palace is even more beautiful than mine. There cannot be two kings in one kingdom. Either I must yield to you, or you must yield to me. I propose that we have a contest. The true test of a king's wealth is how much silk he owns. Tomorrow morning we will have a competition to compare and see who has more silk, you or me. If you win, the whole kingdom and everything in it will be yours, and I will become your servant. But if I win, everything that you have will belong to me, and you will be my servant." The Dream Eater really had no choice, so he agreed to the king's terms.

After the king had gone, the Dream Eater said to Saledam, "This is terrible. The king has hundreds of yards of silk, and we don't have any at all. This is a contest that we will surely lose."

Saledam replied, "If only you would listen to me, things would not be this bad. You keep disregarding what I tell you to do, and things get worse all the time. Now this is a bad situation, but it is not as bad as all that. We can take care of it, but you must do exactly as I say.

"This evening, you must take the treasure box that I hid the light in and throw it into the water of the Marble Rock Pool. As you do so, call out, 'Uncle Naga King, this box was very useful but now we don't need it anymore. Please give me a box of silk.' And a box of silk will float up to the surface of the water, but it is very important that you do not open it until I tell you to."

The Dream Eater agreed to do exactly what Saledam had

told him to do. He took the box in which she had hidden the light and threw it into the water of the Marble Rock Pool. As he did, he called out, "Uncle Naga King, this box was very useful but now we don't need it anymore. Please give me a box of silk." A box of silk floated up to the surface of the water, and he carried it back to the palace. But when he got there, he thought, "This box is so small, I don't see how it could possibly hold enough silk to do us any good. I'd better look and see." So he opened the lid just a tiny crack to peer inside. Immediately a bolt of silk shot out through the crack and started to wind itself around his body like a python.

His terrified shouts brought Saledam running, and with great difficulty she managed to stuff the silk back inside again. "Don't open it again until I tell you to," she said.

When they woke up the next morning, the king was already standing in the courtyard of their palace, with a broad smile on his face. He pointed to one side, and they saw that during the night the king's servants had covered an entire mountain with silk. "Would you like to compare your wealth of silk with mine?" the king said, confidently.

"Yes, wait just a moment and I will get it," said the Dream Eater, going back inside the house.

"Open the box now," said Saledam, and immediately bolts of silk flew in all directions. When the storm of silk had calmed down, they saw that not only had all of the king's silk on the mountain been covered over by the Dream Eater's silk, but it also covered the entire valley and the surrounding countryside as far as the eye could see.

The king was furious. "I refuse to accept the result of this contest," he said. "We must have another one. The true test of a king's dignity is how many yaks he owns. Tomorrow we will compare your herd of yaks and mine. The same agreement will apply.

If you win, the whole kingdom and everything in it will be yours, and I will become your servant. But if I win, everything that you have will belong to me, and you will be my servant."

This was a big problem, for as the Dream Eater knew very well, the king had thousands of yaks. In that pious Buddhist kingdom, it was the custom of the people to buy white yaks that were about to be killed by a butcher and release them as an act of religious merit. Yaks that were rescued in that way were called redeemed yaks, and they were given to the king, who let them graze freely in the royal pastures for the rest of their natural lives. The king had been on the throne for many years, and so of course there were thousands of redeemed white yaks in the royal herds.

"This is terrible," said the Dream Eater. "The king has thousands of yaks, and we don't even have a single yak hair. We are sure to lose everything we have."

"It's a problem, but it's not a big problem," said Saledam. "Here's what you must do. This evening, take the box that the silk was in and throw it into the water of the Marble Rock Pool. As you do so, call out, 'Uncle Naga King, this silk box was very useful but now we don't need it anymore. Please give me a yak box.' And a yak box will float up to the surface of the water, but it is very important that you do not open it until I tell you to."

The Dream Eater once again agreed to do exactly what Saledam had told him to do. He took the box that had contained the silk and threw it into the water of the Marble Rock Pool. As he did, he called out, "Uncle Naga King, this silk box was very useful but now we don't need it anymore. Please give me a yak box." A box that he thought might contain a yak (although he couldn't see how) floated up to the surface of the water, and he carried it back to the palace. This time he did not try to open the box.

The next morning when they woke up, they looked outside and saw that their palace was surrounded by thousands of beautiful white yaks, yaks as far as the eye could see, all pushing against each other and butting up against the palace walls. "Now, husband," said Saledam, "before you open the box you must say to it, 'Yak, your duty is to knock down or chase away all of the yaks that you see around my palace.'"

So the Dream Eater bent down to the box and whispered close to the lid, "Yak, your duty is to knock down or chase away all of the yaks that you see around my palace." Then he opened the lid and immediately there sprang from the box a monster yak, the biggest yak that had ever been seen in the world. Just its head was bigger than any normal yak. The monster yak charged out the palace gate and began goring the yaks from the king's herd, knocking down hundreds of them in one fierce charge. The rest of the yaks were terrified and ran away, down the valley, over the mountains, and out of sight.

A little while later the king and his guards came to the Dream Eater's palace. The king expected to win this contest easily, and he was shocked to see that many of his yaks were lying dead in the field and the others were nowhere to be seen. "Here is my yak," said the Dream Eater, smiling. "Where are yours?"

The king was furious. "This is not fair," he shouted. "Something is going on here. I refuse to accept this. We must have another contest. After all, the true honor of a kingdom is its horses. Tomorrow you and I shall have a horse race, and the winner will be the one and only king. If you win, the whole kingdom and everything in it will be yours, and I will become your servant. But if I win, everything that you have will belong to me, and you will be my servant." And then the king returned to his palace.

"What will we do now?" said the Dream Eater. "Everyone knows that the king is a famous horseman, and we don't own any horses at all. And I'm not a very good rider."

"We've dealt with problems like this one before," said Saledam. "Here's what you must do. This evening, take the box that the yak was in and throw it into the water of the Marble Rock Pool. As you do so, call out, 'Uncle Naga King, this yak box was very useful but now we don't need it anymore. Please give me a horse box.' And a horse box will float up to the surface of the water, but it is very important that you do not open it until I tell you to."

The Dream Eater once again agreed to do exactly what Saledam had told him to do. He took the box that had contained the monster yak and threw it into the water of the Marble Rock Pool. As he did, he called out, "Uncle Naga King, this yak box was very useful but now we don't need it anymore. Please give me a horse box." A box floated up to the surface of the water, and the Dream Eater was sure that it must contain a horse. He carried the box back to the palace and did not try to open it.

The next morning, the king arrived with some of his guards. The shepherd had also come along to watch the great race. The king was mounted on a beautiful horse and wore handsome leather and iron armor; he looked every bit like a great champion. "Are you ready for the race?" he said to the Dream Eater.

"I will just get my horse," said the Dream Eater, going inside his palace.

There Saledam said to him, "Before you open the box, say to the horse, 'Horse, your duty is to overtake the king's horse in three strides.'"

So he bent down close to the box and said softly, "Horse, your duty is to overtake the king's horse in three strides." Then he opened the box and out sprang a magnificent horse, tall and glossy, a horse with the soul of a magical *garuda* bird that could run as if it were flying.

As the Dream Eater was leading the horse outside, Saledam said to him, "After the king names the finish line, the race will start. Let the king go first, and let him get a very big head start. Wait until he has passed the halfway mark before you leave the starting line."

As the king and the Dream Eater, mounted on their horses, walked up to the starting line, the king pointed to a peak in the distance. "That mountain is the finish line," he said. "Get ready to begin."

A moment later, one of the king's guards waved a flag, the signal for the race to start. The king's horse plunged forward and was soon far in the distance. The Dream Eater sat calmly on his horse, watching the king's progress. When the king had passed the bottom of the valley and was starting up the opposite slope, the Dream Eater just touched the *garuda* horse with his whip. The horse soared through the air—one step, two steps, three—passing the king's horse as if it were standing still and arriving first at the finish line.

"Well, I'm surprised," said the Dream Eater.

"What did you say?" said the king.

"I'm surprised that my horse was able to beat yours in just three strides."

"What do you mean by that? Don't you know your own horse? How can you be surprised?" shouted the king, rapidly growing very angry again. "I insist that you explain to me what you mean by that. Something very strange has been going on around here. If you can't give me a good explanation, I'll go to war with you."

The Dream Eater just managed to mumble "I'll talk to you about it tomorrow," and he returned to his palace. All of his joy in winning the race had given way to anxiety that he soon would be at war with the king.

The Dream Eater returned home and told Saledam what had just happened. The shepherd heard the story, too, and he said to

the Dream Eater, "Leave it to me. I'll talk to the king this afternoon and smooth things over for you." The Dream Eater thanked
him and said he thought that was a good idea.

That afternoon, the shepherd went to the royal audience hall
to see the king. "Don't worry about what the Dream Eater said,
Your Majesty," said the shepherd. "He didn't mean anything by
it. I think he was just pretending to be surprised that he won the
race. Of course he knew his own horse and knew that he was bound
to win."

"You mean that he dared to make fun of the king?" the angry
monarch shouted. "He is insolent as well as arrogant? That Dream
Eater has been nothing but trouble for me for a long time, and I
am going to rid myself of his annoying presence." With that, the
king sent the shepherd away and gave orders to his generals to prepare to attack the Dream Eater at dawn the next day.

When he heard what had happened, the Dream Eater said to
Saledam, "I'm afraid the shepherd has just made things worse.
Now we certainly will be attacked by the king's army, and everything that I have will be taken from me, if I even survive the war
itself."

"Don't worry so much," said Saledam. "This is not the hardest problem we have ever faced together. Here's what you must do.
This evening, take the box that the horse was in and throw it into
the water of the Marble Rock Pool. As you do so, call out, 'Uncle
Naga King, this horse box was very useful but now we don't need
it anymore. Please give me an iron man box.' And an iron man
box will float up to the surface of the water. Of course you must
not open it."

Just as before, the Dream Eater agreed to do what Saledam
told him to do. He took the box that had contained the *garuda*
horse and threw it into the water of the Marble Rock Pool. As he
did, he called out, "Uncle Naga King, this horse box was very use-

ful but now we don't need it anymore. Please give me an iron man box." A box floated up to the surface of the water, which the Dream Eater knew must contain an iron man. He carried the box back to the palace; it was very heavy.

The next morning when the Dream Eater and Saledam woke up, they could hear the great army of the king marching up the valley toward their palace. "Here is what you must say to the iron man before you open the box," said Saledam. "Say, 'Here are your orders, iron man. First you must find the shepherd and bash his head in with your iron hammer. Next you must attack the generals and the troops, and make them run away. Finally you should catch the king himself and beat him. You may beat him as much as you please; you may beat him almost to death if you'd like, but you may not kill him.'"

So the Dream Eater bent down to the box and said in a loud voice, like that of a military commander, "Here are your orders, iron man. First you must find the shepherd and bash his head in with your iron hammer. Next you must attack the generals and the troops, and make them run away. Finally you should catch the king himself and beat him. You may beat him as much as you please; you may beat him almost to death if you'd like, but you may not kill him."

Then the Dream Eater opened the box and out stepped a huge giant made entirely of iron. His iron muscles bulged, his iron legs were like tree trunks, and in his huge right hand he carried an iron hammer. He stepped quickly toward the king's army, and spotting the shepherd among a group of soldiers, he swung his iron hammer and hit the shepherd on the head, bashing in his brains and killing him on the spot. Then he began hitting the generals and the soldiers, but they were so afraid that they all began to run away, and he let them go. Many of the soldiers were wounded from blows of the great hammer, but the shepherd was the only one who was killed because he had caused so much trouble for the Dream Eater and Saledam.

The king ran away, too, when he saw that his army was deserting him in the field, and the iron man chased him all the way back to his palace. The iron man stormed into the throne room, seized the king, and began to beat him without mercy. The king shouted, "Stop, stop, you're killing me," but the iron man did not stop until the king was broken and bloody and beaten almost to death.

"I give up," said the king. "I won't fight anymore. The Dream Eater has won. Everything that I owned belongs to him now, and I am his servant. And I will give my daughter to him as his queen, because he spared my life. But I must say, I am really surprised."

"What did you say?" asked the iron man.

"I'm surprised he was able to beat me. I never expected that to happen."

"Then you have your answer," said the iron man. And he turned to walk back to the palace to tell the Dream Eater what the king had said.

So the Dream Eater moved into the royal palace, and all of the treasures in the king's treasure boxes belonged to him. He had two wives, the *naga* Princess Saledam and Princess Palmo, the old king's daughter. The two queens became very good friends, and they loved and supported each other just as they loved and supported the Dream Eater. Each of them had a baby and when they became pregnant again, everyone in the kingdom rejoiced at the royal family's good fortune.

THE LONG STORY had made the miles go quickly, and Nagarjuna's cave was almost in sight when Ngudup Dorjee reached the story's end. "So you see," said Ngudup Dorjee, "dreams really do come true sometimes."

"Yes, I see that now," said Dersang, happily. Before the first word had passed his lips, the leather strap broke, the bag burst open, and Ngudup Dorjee was rushing back toward the old cemetery again. He didn't forget to give Dersang a little slap on the cheek as he flew past.

The Boy Who Understood Animals

Once upon a time, there was a rich family that lived in a beautiful mountain valley in Tibet. Their valley was full of grassy meadows, and in those meadows the family kept sheep. There were hundreds of sheep because the valley was very green and the family was very wealthy.

To look after the sheep, the family employed a young boy from a poor family who lived in the village in the valley. His name was Tenzin, and he was a very good boy. Sometimes he could be naughty, and sometimes he was even hot-tempered, but most of the time he was kind and cheerful. He was particularly well suited to being a shepherd because he liked animals very much and did not mind being alone with them all day.

In a hillside above the meadows where the sheep grazed was a cave. Tenzin happened to discover the entrance to the cave one day, and soon it became his favorite place. He could relax there, out of the hot sun, and keep an eye on all of the sheep spread out in the meadows below. He got into the habit of eating his lunch in the cave every day, and sometimes he went exploring in the inner part of the cave just to see what he could see. Much to his surprise, he found, deep within the cave, an old stone statue of the Buddha.

Tenzin thought the statue was very beautiful, in fact probably the most beautiful manmade thing he had ever seen. It had a serene, calm face and covering its body were carved folds of cloth that looked more like silk than stone. But the statue was also very dirty because the cave was home to a huge flock of swifts—night-flying, insect-eating birds that soiled everything below their nests on the roof of the cave.

Soon Tenzin made a point of bringing with him to the cave every day an old cloth and an extra jar of water. When he had finished his lunch, he would carefully wash the statue of the Buddha, cleaning off all of the mess that the birds had made the night before. He didn't quite know why he did so, but it seemed important and right, and he cleaned the Buddha statue every day for a long time.

One day, he had just finished making the statue clean again when he was aware of a voice speaking to him. He didn't hear the voice with his ears exactly, but he understood it in his heart.

"Young man," said the voice, "you have been very good to me for a long time now, and so I am going to reward you for your faithful service. Think carefully of some attainment that you would like to have, and then pray to the Buddha. You will not receive it right away, but when your heart is sufficiently filled with compassion, then the attainment will be yours."

Tenzin did not have to think for very long because there was already something that he had always wanted to be able to do. And so he prayed to the Buddha:

"I am with my master's sheep every day, and all day they say to me, 'Baaa, baaa.' I think they are trying to talk to me, but I don't understand their language. And I hear the birds in the meadow singing to me, 'Cheep, cheep, kukkuru,' and I know that they are talking to me, too, but I don't know what they are saying. What I would like is to understand the language of animals."

"This attainment will be yours," said the voice, and then there was silence.

Tenzin walked out of the cave into the meadow, and he heard the sheep all around him. But it still just sounded like "baaa, baaa," and he couldn't understand anything that they were saying. He wondered if the whole thing had been only a dream, and after awhile he didn't think anything more about it.

SOMETIME LATER, the rich family that owned the sheep was planning a big party to celebrate the wedding of one of their sons. The wedding banquet of course would include a roasted sheep, but they didn't know which of their many sheep to kill for this purpose. One of the uncles in the family suggested asking the shepherd boy.

"But I don't know either," Tenzin said. "How could I choose which sheep to kill?"

"Well," the uncle said, "for example, perhaps there is one particular sheep that gives you a lot of trouble and that you would like to get rid of. This would solve two problems at once: the wedding guests would have a nice sheep to eat, and your life as a shepherd would become easier."

"Now that you mention it," said Tenzin, "there is one very troublesome sheep that often makes me lose my temper. She wanders away from the meadow, and I have to go and find her; when we move from one meadow to another, she always dawdles behind and I have to go back and fetch her. Yes, if you kill that sheep, my life certainly would be much easier."

"Fine," said the uncle. "That's settled, then. We'll slaughter her tomorrow morning."

That night, though, Tenzin was not able to get to sleep at all. "What have I done?" he thought. "I feel like a murderer. By picking out that sheep to be killed, it is just as if I were killing her myself. And what has she ever really done that's so bad? And even if she does give me trouble sometimes, she has a lamb now, and if the mother is killed the lamb will certainly die also. Surely the lamb has never done me any harm."

Without quite knowing why, he got up from his bed, crept out of the house without waking up his parents, and walked very quietly down into the valley where the sheep were all huddled together for the night in a big fenced-in pen. Looking them over, he soon found the doomed mother sheep and was heartbroken to see tears streaming down her cheeks.

Suddenly Tenzin realized that he was hearing not just "baaa, baaa" anymore, but the actual voices of the sheep in the pen. Compassion had been awakened in his heart, and so the condition that the Buddha had placed on his prayer had been fulfilled. He had achieved the attainment he wanted of being able to understand the language of animals.

As he listened carefully, Tenzin heard the high, quavering voice of the little lamb.

"Mother, why are you crying?"

"Hush, little one," said the mother sheep. "Don't talk now. Use the time to drink as much of my milk as you can, because after tomorrow there will be no more for you."

"But, Mother, how can that be?"

"Tomorrow morning, my little child, I will be killed and turned into meat for a feast. I don't think that I have done anything very wrong, but the shepherd has picked me out to be killed. This must be a fulfillment of my own karma. I only hope that you will be able to survive when I am gone." Tears were pouring from her eyes then, and the lamb and the shepherd boy were crying, too.

Suddenly Tenzin called out, "Stop, stop. I can't stand it anymore. What can I do to save you from this terrible end? I feel like I'm killing you myself."

"We could try running away together," suggested the mother sheep.

"Yes," said Tenzin, his face brightening again. "That's what we must do, even though I know that if we run away, some other sheep will have to die instead of you. I can't control the fate of every sheep, but I can avoid selecting a fellow creature to be deliberately killed. Come over here by the fence where I can pick you up, and we'll leave right now."

So the boy lifted the sheep and the lamb out of the pen, and they walked together up to the head of the valley and over the mountains beyond. They never looked back. They walked for many days until they were far away from the valley where they had lived.

One day they reached a very small valley with a small green meadow and a pool of clear, clean water. Above the meadow was a small cave, rather like the cave Tenzin had enjoyed in their old home. And right away he knew that this was where they were meant to stop. They moved into the cave together and lived there for many weeks, far away from the rest of the world. The valley was full of birds and wild animals, and Tenzin talked with all of them and was very happy.

Without Tenzin knowing it, one day some hunters came to the valley. He was sitting at the entrance to the cave, chatting with some birds; the sheep and the lamb were grazing in the little meadow down below. The hunters decided that the boy was enchanted and they didn't want to risk coming close to him, so they went quietly away again.

It happened that the valley where Tenzin was living was within the boundaries of a great kingdom, though of course the boy knew nothing at all about that. The kingdom was ruled by a king who was not only rich and powerful, but also wise and just. But neither the king's power nor his wisdom seemed to do him

any good, for he suddenly had been stricken with the greatest sorrow that can happen to anyone: his beloved only child was on the
verge of death. His daughter, Princess Lhamo, was sweet and beautiful, intelligent and kind; she was the great joy of her father's
heart. But for many days now she had been lying in bed deathly
ill, and although the king consulted every doctor in his kingdom
and invited famous doctors from all of the surrounding kingdoms
as well, none of them could diagnose her illness or do anything to
make it improve. Instead, every day the princess seemed to grow
weaker and weaker, until her death seemed only days away.

Finally, in desperation, the king issued a decree saying that
anyone who could cure his daughter would be given half of the
kingdom as a reward. This, of course, brought out a huge crowd
of magicians and quacks who chanted every kind of chant that had
ever been heard, and dosed the princess with every herb and pill
and syrup that had ever been tasted, and made her hot, or cold, or
damp, or dry; in short, they did everything possible to make life
miserable for the poor dying princess without doing anything to
cure her illness.

Just then the hunters thought of the strange boy they had
seen in the little valley on the far edge of the kingdom. "He surely
is enchanted," they said to one another. "Perhaps he has some
strange art that will help our beautiful princess." So they went to
the court to tell the king, who immediately sent officers to fetch
the boy and bring him to the palace.

When the officers arrived in the valley, the shepherd boy was
terrified of them because he thought they had come to arrest him
for stealing the sheep and the lamb. Even when he understood
what they wanted, he refused to listen to them. He certainly did
not want to leave his valley and go off with them, no matter how
they pleaded. But finally they said, "Listen. This is not a matter
of your choice. If there is any possibility that you can help the

princess, you must come with us. Come on your own two feet if you will, or we will carry you if you will not walk, but you must come to the king's palace without delay."

Given no real choice, Tenzin went with the officers. The walk from the valley to the royal capital city took several days, but finally they arrived at the gate of the palace. Just inside the gate was a waiting room, and the officers said to Tenzin, "Wait here while we tell the king that you have arrived and see what he wants to do with you."

As he was waiting, he noticed a mother cat playing with her kitten in the corner of the room. And, of course, he could understand what they were saying, so he kept very quiet and listened.

"Mother, why are you looking so sad?" asked the kitten.

"I'm sad because Princess Lhamo is so ill, and she is probably going to die. I will miss her very much. She always paid attention to me and liked to play with me and let me sleep on her bed. And what makes me saddest of all is that she does not need to die, but these humans do not know how to take care of her."

"Mother, how can that be? She has been seen by so many doctors. How could they fail to cure her if she can be cured?"

"It is because they do not know what to look for. The cause of her illness is very simple, but they are not aware of it."

"Then, Mother, how do you know what it is?"

"I know because I saw it happen. One day, when Princess Lhamo was taking a nap, I saw a spider crawl into her ear. I was not close enough to catch it before it got into her ear, and once it was inside there was no way for me to get it out. It is a terrible, poisonous spider, and now it has gone deeper and deeper into her ear. Worse than that, it has laid eggs in there, and they have hatched, and the baby spiders have found their way into her brain. That is what is making her ill, and that is why she is likely to die."

"Mother, my paw is still very small. Maybe I could reach into her ear and catch the spider and pull it out."

"You are very good, my dear, and I am proud of you for thinking of that. But it wouldn't work. It would only drive the spider deeper inside, and Princess Lhamo would die even sooner. You and I cannot get the spiders out, but if the humans understood what the problem was, they could do it."

The boy sat very, very still, hardly daring to breathe for fear that he would interrupt what the cat was saying. The officers might be coming back for him at any moment. Would there be time for him to learn the secret?

"Mother, do you know how to get the spiders out?" the kitten asked.

"They can't be pulled out, but they can be lured out," answered the mother cat. "The only way to do it would be to trick them with sweet music."

"How would music do any good?"

"Spiders after all eat insects. When spiders are hiding in a garden, they listen for the songs of birds because birds eat insects too. When many birds are singing all at once, the spiders know that it is because the garden is full of insects and the birds have come to feast on them. So the spiders come out of hiding and eat the insects that the birds overlook.

"If humans would play music like the sounds of birds around the princess's bed, the spiders would be fooled and would come out of her ear, expecting to find a feast. And when they had come out it would be possible then to put a drop of sweet, warm oil in her ear so they could not go back again. And then the princess would be cured.

"I have tried over and over again to explain to the humans exactly what should be done. But of course we cannot understand their language, and they cannot understand ours. All they hear when I talk to them is 'meow, meow,' and when they reply to us, all we hear is 'blah, blah, blah.' Meanwhile Princess Lhamo gets more and more ill, and no one knows how to cure her."

Just then the officers came back to tell Tenzin that the king was ready to see him. He followed them into the throne room.

"Well, young shepherd, it may be that you are our last hope," said the king. "Do you think you can do the princess any good?"

"Your Majesty, I know exactly how to cure her illness," said Tenzin. "But what I need to do may sound very strange to you. I ask that you please follow my instructions, even if they don't seem to make much sense to you."

"I'm ready to try anything," said the king. "Ask for whatever you need, and I will see that it is done."

"Then," said the shepherd, "the first thing you must do is surround the princess's bed with vases of flowers and flowering plants growing in pots. Her bedroom must become like a garden."

"Consider it done," said the king. "What else to you need?"

"Next you must issue an urgent call for all the best musicians and singers in the kingdom to come to the palace at once. We especially need those who know how to imitate the calls of birds.

"Also you must have one of the servants prepare a small jar of scented oil, warmed to a comfortable temperature. Bring this oil and a small spoon into the princess's bedroom, but don't do anything with it until I say what to do."

The king gave all of the necessary orders, and within a very short time Princess Lhamo's room was filled with flowers and musicians and singers, and a maidservant holding a small jar of oil and a spoon.

"Now," said Tenzin to the musicians and singers, "you must all play and sing as sweetly as you can, imitating every kind of bird whose song has ever been heard. Don't stop until I tell you to."

Immediately the room was turned into a kind of garden of

paradise, with the trilling and cooing and whistling of birds blending together to make music of celestial sweetness. And the musicians were horrified to see as they played and sang, a dark hairy spider crawl out of the princess's ear, followed by a parade of baby spiders of the same kind. In fact, some of them were almost too disgusted to continue with their music, but Tenzin glared at them and they quickly went back to their duties.

When Tenzin was sure that the last of the baby spiders had emerged, he said to the serving-maid, "Quickly, now, use the spoon to put several drops of oil in the princess's ear. The spiders will soon realize that we've tricked them into coming out, but the oil will keep them from getting back in again." So that was done and meanwhile the cat and the kitten, who had been watching everything with surprise (how had the humans finally figured things out?) pounced on the spiders and tore them all to shreds.

As soon as the warm, scented oil touched her ear, Princess Lhamo began to get better. A soft pink blush colored her cheeks, and her pale lips once again began to turn red. She stirred slightly, like a person whose sleep has been interrupted.

"We must leave her alone now," said Tenzin. "She will recover quickly on her own. In a few days, she will be well."

When they had returned to the throne room, the king gathered together all of his ministers and officers and commanded the shepherd boy to kneel before him.

"My boy," said the king, "you have done what no one else has been able to do. Thanks to you, my beloved princess's life has been saved. I insist on rewarding you by giving you half of my kingdom."

"I am very grateful to you, Your Majesty," said the shepherd, "but I cannot accept such a reward. A good deed that is done to earn a reward is worth very little; my only intention was to save

Princess Lhamo's life. I was not thinking about a reward, and I don't want to accept one."

"No, no," said the king. "That really will not do. You cannot deprive me of the pleasure of rewarding you when you have done so much for me. If you will not take half of my kingdom, then name some other reward instead."

"What I would really like," said Tenzin, "would be to be allowed to kiss the princess's hand when she is all better."

"That you surely shall do," said the king, "though it does not seem like enough to me."

Princess Lhamo was young and strong, and once the cause of her illness had been removed, she recovered her health very quickly. In just a few days, Tenzin was able to walk quietly into the princess's room to claim his reward. He held her hand in his own and bent his head down to put a gentle kiss on her wrist. Feeling the touch of his lips, the princess opened her eyes and was amazed at what she saw. As the shepherd started to move away from her, she shot out her hand and grabbed him by the arm in a stronger grip than he would have thought possible.

"Father," she said, "who is this handsome young stranger in my room?"

"This," said the king, "is the young man who cured you of your illness when everyone else despaired of your life and who brought you back from the brink of the grave."

"Then, Father," said Princess Lhamo, "you had better make arrangements for me to marry this young man as quickly as possible. At the very moment I opened my eyes and saw his gentle face I fell in love with him, and now I know why. He will be my husband, or I never will have a husband in this life."

"Shepherd, what do you think of this?" asked the king. "Will you accept this as part of your reward?"

"Nothing could please me more, Your Majesty," replied
Tenzin.

So in a very few days, Princess Lhamo and Tenzin were married. He became the crown prince of the kingdom, and he and his
bride were very happy together. After many years the old king
passed away, and Tenzin became king in his turn; and he was as
wise and good as his father-in-law had been, and he seemed to
know things that were beyond the intelligence of ordinary
humans, for he never forgot where he had learned how to save the
princess's life, and he never stopped listening to the animals.

The Cook, the Cat, and the Endless Story

Once there was a king of a very prosperous and peaceful country. The king lived in a grand palace surrounded by as many wonderful and luxurious things as anyone could ever want. But the king's favorite thing in the whole world was not some beautiful and expensive work of art or some rare object that had been brought from far away beyond the seas; the king's favorite thing in the whole world was his cat. She was a pretty, friendly cat, and she used to curl up on the king's lap when he sat on his golden throne dealing with all of the difficult affairs that a king has to take care of. She was a very nice cat, and the king loved her very much.

The king also loved to eat, so one of the most important people in the palace was the royal cook. This cook was the best cook in the whole kingdom, and every day he had to make many different kinds of dishes for the king's table. Now, being the king of a Buddhist country, the king should have been a vegetarian, but he was not; in fact, he loved to eat meat. Some people even said that he must have been a tiger in a previous lifetime. So naturally the cook always had to serve the king a number of dishes that were made of meat.

One day, the cook went to the marketplace in the king's royal city to buy ingredients for that night's dinner, and he discovered to his horror that all of the food stalls had already run out of meat. He went from one food seller to the next, explaining how important it was that he buy meat for the king's dinner, but it didn't do any good. There just wasn't any meat for sale in the market anywhere.

The cook went back to the palace feeling very worried. He knew that if he served the king a meatless supper, the king would be very angry. At best the cook would be fired from his job and thrown out of the palace, and if the king was in a bad mood he might even order the guards to cut the cook's head off. The cook sat in his kitchen feeling very worried and sad, trying to figure out some solution to his problem. And just then the king's cat walked into the kitchen.

"Here, kitty, kitty," said the cook.

The cat ignored him. She sat down and started to wash her face with her paws.

"Here, kitty, kitty," said the cook. "Nice kitty."

The cat walked over to the cook and rubbed herself against his legs.

"Nice kitty," said the cook, reaching down to pet her.

The cat started to purr.

Then the cook grabbed the cat, broke her neck, and threw her down on the chopping block so fast that the cat was on her way to her next lifetime before she even quite realized what had happened.

Killing the cat was, of course, a very mean and terrible thing for the cook to do, but he was a desperate man. He thought, "Either I kill the cat or the king will kill me"; and given the predicament he was in, it's easy to see why he made the choice that he did.

Anyway, what's done was done, and the cook cut the cat up into little pieces and cooked the meat with a lot of fragrant, delicious spices. And the king had meat for dinner after all.

Later that night, the king called for the cook to come into the royal dining room.

"That was a new kind of meat that you served to me tonight," said the king. "It was really delicious. What was it?"

"Oh, it was nothing special, Your Majesty," answered the cook. "Just a little something that I whipped up on the spur of the moment."

"That may be," said the king, "but what kind of meat was it? I might want to have it again sometime, and I'd like to know what to ask for."

"Well, Your Majesty, actually I'd rather not say," answered the cook. "You might call it a trade secret, I suppose. If you want this particular dish again, you could just tell me that you'd like some 'special meat,' and I'll know what you mean."

"What?" roared the king. "Do you dare to defy me? I asked you to tell me what kind of meat that was, and you refuse? Tell me right away or I'll see that you'll regret it."

"Really, Your Majesty, I do beg to be excused," said the cook. "But I'm afraid that if I were to answer your question, you might be very angry with me."

"Nonsense," said the king. "Don't be absurd. Why would I be angry? I just want to know what it is that I ate this evening. And anyway it's my palace, you're my cook, and you have to do what I say. I demand that you answer my question right now."

"I will if you insist, Your Majesty," said the cook. "But only if you promise that you won't be angry with me."

"Very well," said the king. "I don't see what all the fuss is about."

"Do you promise, in front of all these people," said the cook, "that you won't punish me after I've answered your question?"

"I've already said so," shouted the king. "I promise. Now tell me. What was that meat?"

"Well, actually," said the cook, "you see, that meat, so to speak, that meat, in fact, Your Majesty, that meat was your cat."

"What!" screamed the king, with his eyes bulging out of his head. "How dare you! I can't believe it. You killed my cat? You *cooked* my cat? Monster! Idiot! Murderer! Guards!" said the king, "cut this man's head off immediately."

"Wait, Your Majesty," cried the terrified cook. "You promised."

"Well, I don't promise anymore," said the king. "I take back my promise. I had no idea you were such a monster. Why shouldn't I have your head cut off right here and now?"

"But, Your Majesty, everyone heard you give that promise. You can't take it back, or no one will ever believe you again." The cook began to think that he might get out of this alive after all.

"Very well," said the king. "I won't cut your head off, at least not right now, but that doesn't mean that you can get away with this either. You killed my cat, and that means that you are going to have to take her place. I know I won't be able to bear to think about my poor cat, so your job will be to distract me for the rest of my life. So here is your punishment: starting tomorrow, you must tell me a story that has no ending. It had better be a good story, and if it ever comes to an end, your life will end that very same day. Now get out of my sight."

The cook went home, looking and feeling miserable. The minute he came in the door, his wife said to him, "Darling, what's wrong? You look as though you've had a terrible day today."

"You can't even imagine how terrible it was," said the cook. And he told his wife the whole story of what had happened. "So I think I'm really finished," said the cook. "No matter what kind of story I make up, sooner or later it will come to an end, and then the king will chop off my head after all."

The cook's wife thought for a few minutes and then said, "Well, my love, I admit that things look pretty bad right now. But don't give up. If you do what I tell you to do, the king will beg you to stop talking long before you come to the end of your story, and then your problems will be over. When you go to the palace tomorrow, this is what you should say. . . ."

THE NEXT morning, the cook went to the palace and very nervously walked up to the king, who was sitting on his golden throne and feeling in a very bad mood without his nice little cat curled up in his lap.

"You may begin," said the king. "And this had better be good."

"Tell me, Your Majesty," began the cook, "have you ever noticed that there is something in the world more powerful than yourself?"

"Never," replied the king. "In fact, I think it is quite ridiculous to imagine that there is anything more powerful than I. After all, I am the king."

"True," said the cook, "and as far as we know you are the most powerful king in the entire world. Yet I dare to suggest that there is something more powerful than you."

"Then what is it?" asked the king.

"The sky," said the cook. "Because no matter how high you are, Your Majesty, the sky is always above you, and doesn't that mean it is more powerful than you?"

"Are you suggesting, Cook, that the sky is the most powerful thing in the whole world?"

"Not at all, Your Majesty," replied the cook. "For there is something more powerful even than the sky."

"Oh?" said the king. "What is that?"

"Clouds, Your Majesty," said the cook. "Because when the sky is covered with clouds, then no matter how high and bright the sky may be, it cannot be seen. And so clouds are clearly more powerful than the sky."

"Does that mean that clouds are the most powerful thing in the universe?" asked the king. "That seems rather strange."

"Not exactly, Your Majesty," replied the cook. "There is something even more powerful than clouds."

"What could that be?"

"The wind, Your Majesty. When the wind blows, it scatters the clouds in all directions, and there is nothing they can do to resist its force. Therefore I say that the wind is even more powerful than the clouds."

"Is there anything more powerful than the wind, then?" asked the king, who was beginning to see that this story really might go on forever.

"Actually, there is," said the cook. "And what is more powerful than the wind is a wall. You may have noticed this yourself. When the wind blows against a strong wall, such as one of the brick walls of your palace, for example, it is turned back by its strength. Indeed, compared to the strength of a strong wall, the strength of the wind is nothing. So a wall is clearly more powerful than the wind."

"I suppose that now you will tell me there is something more powerful than a wall," said the king.

"Yes, indeed," said the cook. "But what it is will surprise you. A mouse is more powerful than a wall."

"How can that possibly be?"

"Consider that a mouse, using only its sharp teeth and its tiny paws, can dig tunnels under the strongest wall, and when enough mice dig enough tunnels, the wall collapses of its own weight, no matter how strong it once was. If you look at it this way, a mouse is powerful enough to bring down the walls even of a great city."

"I see how that could be true," said the king. "But surely there must be something more powerful than a mouse."

"Of course there is," replied the cook. "Everyone knows that cats eat mice, and so a cat is obviously more powerful than a mouse."

"Oh?" said the king, growing a bit angry at being reminded of cats. "And what would you say is more powerful than a cat?"

"I am," said the cook, "because I killed a cat and cooked it for the king's dinner."

"And I am the king," the king shouted, "and I am most definitely more powerful than you, Cook. In fact, I am powerful enough to have your head cut off right now. What do you think about that?"

"But, Your Majesty," said the cook, "you really mustn't do that. You certainly are more powerful than I am, but keep in mind that there is something still more powerful than you."

"And what might that be?" growled the king.

"The sky," said the cook. "Because no matter how high you are . . ."

"Stop!" shouted the king. "I see what you're doing, and I can't stand it anymore. Stop this stupid story right now. And just to live up to my part of the bargain, I won't cut your head off after all, but get out of my sight this minute. I never want to see you again."

"DID IT work?" asked the cook's wife.

"It was perfect," said the cook. "We're safe now."

THE NEXT morning, the king sent a messenger to the cook's house.

"The king orders you to come to the palace right away," said the messenger.

"Now what?" thought the cook, as he hurried to the palace. As soon as he arrived, he was brought to the royal audience chamber, where the king sat on his golden throne.

"Cook," said the king, "I have been thinking."

"Yes, Your Majesty?" said the cook in a trembling voice.

"Yes. And I have decided that you are much too smart to remain a cook. I am still angry at you for killing my cat, but that was also partly my fault because of my greedy appetite for meat. So I have decided to forgive you. And because you were so clever with your story yesterday, I am going to make you chief minister of my kingdom so you can put your talents to better use."

"Thank you very much, Your Majesty," answered the cook. "But then I must confess that what I said yesterday wasn't really my own idea. My wife told me what to say, so she should get the credit for it."

"Really?" said the king. "Then your wife must be an extraordinary woman. You both must move into the palace immediately. I will make your wife my adopted sister, and you will be my chief minister, and with the help of the two of you my kingdom will become richer and stronger than ever."

And that is what happened. The cook's wife became the king's sister, and he always listened to her advice. The cook became the king's chief minister, and everyone thought that he was the cleverest talker who ever lived. And they were all quite happy.

The Boy Who Never Lied

"He did it again, Lord Nagarjuna," said Dersang, sadly.

"You mean *you* did it again," replied the old philosopher. "I suppose he told you another story."

"Yes, and it was so exciting I made a comment out loud before I knew what I was doing," said the boy.

"You really must stop listening to Ngudup Dorjee's stories," said Nagarjuna. "He is very good at telling them, and you should know that he intends to trick you every time. I suppose we should thank him for the valuable lessons he's giving you in self-control, but that doesn't get us any closer to capturing him and turning him into a lump of gold.

"Anyway, what's done is done. Here's a fresh container of food, a new sack, and your axe. Off you go now. Come back with the bag full this time, if you can."

When Dersang reached the cemetery, he had no trouble at all finding Ngudup Dorjee and chasing him up a tree. "Ngudup Dorjee," he called, "will you come down now, or do I need to chop your tree down?"

"No, no, you've got me again," said Ngudup Dorjee, climbing down the tree.

Dersang seized the spirit by the scruff of the neck, flung him

into the sack, and fastened the leather strap. Setting off for Nagarjuna's cave again, he had an uneasy feeling he knew what would
happen next.

"Well, boy," said Ngudup Dorjee, "it seems to me that a
story will be just the thing to pass the time along the way. Will
you tell one, or shall I?" When Dersang did not reply, the spirit
said in a cranky voice, "Well, it looks like I will have to do all the
work again. I'll tell you a story about a boy rather like yourself, a
boy who is poor but very honest—in fact, a boy who never lied."

ONCE THERE were two kingdoms that were neighbors. They were
small, rich, peaceful kingdoms, and their kings were good friends.
The ruler of the western kingdom was King Ngawang, and the
ruler of the eastern kingdom was King Sonam. Because the two
royal capital cities were not far apart, the kings often visited each
other in their palaces.

The two kings were friends, but they were friendly rivals.
Each of them was very proud of his good taste and artistic judg-
ment, and each of them liked to collect rare and beautiful things.
They were very proud of all of the treasures they had collected over
the years, and they competed to see who could show off the rich-
est and most unusual new item whenever they met.

One day King Ngawang, ruler of the western kingdom,
went to visit the palace of the eastern king, bringing with him his
newest treasure. "Look at this," he said to King Sonam, holding a
cup made of beautifully carved and polished rhinoceros horn. "It
is carved on the inside with exactly one thousand images of the
Buddha. And what is even more remarkable," he went on, holding
the rhino-horn cup to the light, "is that the horn has been polished
to such thinness that when you hold it up to the light, you can see
from the outside the carved Buddha images shining through from

the inside. I think that no one has ever before seen a rhino-horn cup as finely carved as this one."

"That is certainly an extraordinary treasure," said King Sonam. "I think that it is the finest thing that you have ever acquired for your collection of rarities. But," he continued, "I also have recently acquired a new treasure, and I think it is something even more rare than your beautiful rhino-horn cup."

"I think you are just trying to spoil my pleasure," said the western king. "I don't think you really have anything that can compete with this."

"But indeed I have," said King Sonam. "My newest treasure is a servant who never lies. I think you will agree that there is nothing more rare than that."

"If it were true, I would agree," said King Ngawang. "But I don't believe it. I don't think that there has ever been a person who has not told a lie at one time or another."

"Nevertheless, it is true," his friend replied. "This servant is a young stable boy named Tsering. I began to hear about him from my other servants, who were amazed to find such complete honesty in a simple, young peasant boy. So I ordered him brought before me and examined him personally. Sure enough, he gave an honest answer to every question that I asked him. Even when I said to him, 'Tsering, I will kill you right now if you do not tell a lie,' he said to me, 'Very well, Your Majesty, kill me if you wish, but I will not lie to you.' So I believe that he is not capable of telling a lie.

"After that, I put him in charge of my personal horse, the most remarkable horse in my whole kingdom, if not in the whole world, and he has always taken care of him in a completely satisfactory way. He reports to me regularly, and I have never known him to be less than completely truthful."

"Even so, I do not believe that there has ever been a person who is incapable of telling a lie," said King Ngawang. "I will make a bet with you. I believe that within half a year, your young stable boy will be found to have told a lie. If I am right, you must give me half of your kingdom. But if, after six months, this Tsering still has not told a lie, I will give half of my kingdom to you."

"Agreed," said King Sonam. After that, their conversation turned to other things, and later the western king went home after a very pleasant visit with his friend.

Now it happened that King Ngawang had a very beautiful young daughter, Princess Drolker. When he returned home to his own palace in the western kingdom, he called his daughter to him and said, "You can help me to win a wager that will make us much richer than we are now. My neighbor, King Sonam, has a certain stable boy that he claims can never tell a lie. I want you to go to the eastern kingdom and seduce this boy, whose name is Tsering, and when you have done so, you will be able to make him tell a lie. Tsering takes care of the king's favorite horse, and when he is in your power, I'm sure you will find a way to make him lie to the king about that horse. If you can do that, the king will have to give me half of his kingdom."

"Yes, Father, I will do my best," said the princess.

The next morning, the princess went by herself to the eastern kingdom wearing ordinary clothes and walking along the road like a common peasant girl. When she came near the royal stables, she watched until she saw a stable boy taking care of the most beautiful horse of all. She knew that this must be the king's favorite horse, so she said to the boy, "I would like to ask a favor of you. I am on a long journey, and I know that I will not have time to reach my destination before it grows dark tonight. Will you let me sleep in the stable tonight? I promise not to be any trouble, and tomorrow I will go on my way."

Tsering knew of course that he should not allow strangers into the royal stables, but he was so charmed by the girl's beauty and innocent manner that he agreed to let her stay there for the night, and he gave her a bed of clean straw in one of the empty horse stalls.

Later that night, after they had both gone to bed, Tsering could not get to sleep, thinking about the beautiful girl in the stall nearby. And when, in the middle of the night, she silently crept into his bed, he could not resist making love with her. By the time morning arrived, he was completely in love with the mysterious girl.

"I'm really not in a big hurry," she said to him. "I could stay here a few more days if you'd like." Of course, the boy was overjoyed with this idea. Soon the girl seemed to be as much in love with him as he was with her. The days stretched into weeks, and soon Tsering and the beautiful girl (who did not tell Tsering her real name) were living together as man and wife, with no thought of her ever continuing her journey again.

Naturally the stable boy talked sometimes to his wife about his duties, and she learned therefore what a marvelous horse he was taking care of. The king's horse was what is called a *changshe* horse, a name for the most remarkable sort of horse that anyone could imagine. It does not only mean a beautiful horse, though the king's horse was very beautiful. Nor does it mean only a brave and strong horse, though the king's horse could carry the king into combat and fight all day without becoming tired or shying away. A *changshe* horse is beautiful and brave, sure-footed and tireless, spirited but obedient. More than that, it is a friend, companion, and advisor to its human owner, for a *changshe* horse can talk. As her husband (or at least that's how Tsering thought of himself) described this wonderful beast, Princess Drolker understood why her father had said that the horse would provide a way of forcing the boy to lie.

One evening Tsering came back from a long day's work to

find his wife lying in bed, looking deathly ill. Her skin was damp and cold and had turned a pale shade of blue; her breathing was shallow and her eyes were dim. She looked like someone on the verge of death.

"Darling, what has happened?" the boy cried in alarm. "How have you suddenly become so ill?" In fact, the princess was in no danger. She had put into her mouth some glass beads that she had brought with her especially for this purpose; the beads were suffused with a drug that would mimic the effects of a deadly illness but really would do her no harm.

"My husband, I am sorry to say that I'm afraid I will die very soon," said the girl in a weak, fainting voice.

"No, no, that can't be," Tsering said, weeping. "Isn't there anything I can do? There must be something I can do to make this terrible illness leave you again."

"Well, there is one thing," she said. "No, never mind, it would never work. It's impossible. I must die, and there really isn't anything that can be done."

"Darling, you seem afraid to tell me something. What did you want to say? If there is some way to save you, I will do anything at all."

"You see, my love," the girl said, "there is one thing that will cure this deadly disease, but I'm sure you will not be able to bring it about. I will become well again if I am able to eat the heart of a horse."

"Well, we have many horses here," the stable boy said. "I don't see why I couldn't get you the heart of a horse. Can it be just any horse at all?"

"That's the problem," she replied. "It has to be the heart of a *changshe* horse. I know that you are taking care of a *changshe* horse for the king, but you would never be able to kill it and obtain its heart for me, even though that's the only thing that would save my life."

"Oh, dear. That's terrible," said Tsering. "It certainly will be difficult to get the *changshe* horse's heart for you. I would do anything for you, but I don't see how I can do this."

"I told you it was no use," said his wife. "It doesn't matter. Don't think about it anymore. I will die tonight, and I hope that you will sometimes remember me fondly." Then she turned her face to the wall and seemed to fall into a deep, deathly sleep.

Tsering slowly walked back to the stables, thinking, "There is no way around it. Now I must kill my master's favorite horse. I wonder what will happen to me then? But it is the only thing that will cure my wife, and I will do anything for her."

When he reached the stall of the *changshe* horse, he was amazed to find that the horse was crying. He said to the horse, "Why are you crying?" The horse replied that he already knew what had happened, and he knew that the stable boy had come to kill him.

"No, I can't do it," Tsering said, stroking the horse's neck and trying to soothe his tears. "Even if it means that my wife must die, I cannot kill you. Please, I will let you out of the stable, and you must run away. I will tell my wife that you ran away and I ran after you but was not able to catch you. Then perhaps she will die, but you will be safe."

"It's all right," said the horse. "You don't need to kill me, but you can have my heart. Now here is what you must do. Find the most beautiful mare in the king's stables and lead her here to my stall and let her walk before my eyes. Then I will die, and you can take my heart to cure your wife's illness."

So that is what the stable boy did. He led the most beautiful mare in the royal stable to the *changshe* horse's stall. After the *changshe* horse had looked at the mare, he fell dead on the floor. The stable boy wept when his old friend died, but he knew that there was no time to lose. Taking out a long knife, he removed the horse's heart and brought it back to his wife.

"Thank you so much, my love," said the disguised princess. "This will help to cure my illness. But I'm afraid that things have gone so far now that I need to eat the horse's head also. Could you go back and get it for me?"

Doing as he was told, Tsering went back, cut off the horse's head, and brought it back for his wife. Then he returned to the stables once again to clean up the *changshe* horse's stall and lock the door, hoping that no one would notice for awhile that the horse was dead.

When he returned to the room he shared with his wife, he was amazed to find her gone. There was no sign of her, or of her clothes, or of the horse's heart and head; everything had vanished. "This is terrible," said Tsering. "I have brought about the death of my best friend, the *changshe* horse. My wife must be cured of her disease, but now she has run away from me. What shall I do now?

"Next time King Sonam sees me, he certainly will ask how the *changshe* horse is doing, and I will not know what to say. How can I tell him that I cut out the horse's heart and cut off his head? There will be no way to explain it to the king. Even though I have never told a lie before in my life, I think maybe I will have to lie to the king now because I surely cannot tell him the truth.

"But if I am going to lie," said Tsering, "I don't even know how to do it. I'd better find some way to try out what I am going to say."

Then he went to a secret place out in the hills where he knew he would not be disturbed, and there he made a tall pile of rocks to represent the king. He dressed the rock cairn in a suit of clothing and placed bouquets of flowers on either side of it; then he bowed down to the cairn, pretending that it was King Sonam. "Hello, my little stable boy," he made the rock cairn say. "How are you today?"

"I am very well, Your Majesty," the boy replied.

"And how is my favorite *changshe* horse?" the king asked.

"The *changshe* horse, the *changshe* horse . . . that is, the *changshe* horse, Your Majesty, some robbers broke into the stable and took the *changshe* horse away, and we don't know where to find him now."

As soon as the stable boy said that, the rock cairn came tumbling down, and the rocks were scattered everywhere. "Oh dear," thought the boy. "That obviously is no good. I can't say that. Let me try again."

Once again he built a pile of rocks, dressed it in clothing, and placed vases of flowers to each side. "Hello, my little stable boy," the rock cairn said again. "How are you today?"

"I am very well, Your Majesty," the boy replied.

"And how is my favorite *changshe* horse?" asked the cairn, dressed up like King Sonam.

"Oh, Your Majesty, I'm very sorry. I tried so hard to save the life of your horse, but he slipped in the mud and fell and broke his neck, and there was nothing that any of us could do to help him." Immediately again the rock cairn came crashing down to the ground. "No, I cannot lie," said the stable boy. "I must tell the truth. I will practice what I should say to the king."

So he built up the rock cairn yet again, dressed it in clothing, and set vases of flowers on either side. Tsering pretended that the rock cairn spoke once again. "Hello, my little stable boy," it said. "How are you today?"

"I am very well, Your Majesty," the boy replied.

"And how is my favorite *changshe* horse?" the king asked.

"I am very, very sorry, Your Majesty," Tsering replied. "Your *changshe* horse is dead, and I am responsible for his death. A beautiful girl tricked me and cheated me into killing your horse and bringing her his heart and head. So now the girl is gone, your horse is dead, and there is nothing I can say to you to change that." And when he finished, the rock cairn did not fall down. "Now I see what I must do," thought the stable boy, and he walked back to the stable to await a summons from the king.

The next morning, a messenger came looking for him. "Hey, boy," the messenger called. "The king is looking for you. Get down to the palace right away." So the stable boy went to the palace, very afraid of what would happen to him.

When he was led into the throne room, he was surprised to see two kings sitting side by side—not only his own king, King Sonam, but also King Ngawang from the neighboring country to the west. And he was amazed to see, sitting next to the western king, a very beautiful girl: his wife! But now she was not dressed in peasant clothing, but in a beautiful dress, covered with jewelry and pearls. Tsering did not know what to think.

"Hello, my little stable boy," the king said. "How are you today?"

"I am very well, Your Majesty," Tsering replied.

"And how is my favorite *changshe* horse?" the king asked.

"I am very, very sorry, Your Majesty," said Tsering. "Your *changshe* horse is dead, and I am responsible for his death. A beautiful girl tricked me and cheated me into killing your horse and bringing her his heart and head." And he told the king the whole story, and when he had finished, he said, "And that is the girl, sitting up there near you. I am ready to accept any punishment Your Majesty wants to inflict on me."

Just as he was saying this, another stable boy came running from the royal stables into the throne room, saying, "Your Majesty! Your Majesty, there is wonderful news. One of the mares in the stable has just given birth to a foal, and it is *another changshe* horse. It looks just like your old *changshe* horse."

The king turned to his neighbor and said, "You see, I told you that this boy would never lie. I was sure of that, no matter what tricks you might try to play against him. Now you must give me half of your kingdom.

"Let me tell you now what I intend to do," King Sonam continued. "I will adopt this stable boy as my son and give to him the half of your kingdom that I've just won in our bet. And you must marry your daughter, Princess Drolker, to him so that this time they really will be husband and wife. And so the half of your kingdom that you must give me will remain in both your family and mine, and we can continue to live in peace and friendship together."

So that is what was done. Prince Tsering and Princess Drolker were married immediately, and although he was still angry at her for cheating him, really the two of them were very fond of each other, and they soon were getting along very well together once again. And the two kings continued their friendly rivalry for a long time to come.

"WHAT A good policy it is never to tell a lie," said Dersang. And although Dersang tried to duck out of the way, Ngudup Dorjee still managed to slap him on the cheek as he burst out of the sack and went flying back to the cemetery.

King Salgyel's Daughter, Princess Dorjee

A certain kingdom was ruled by a wise and good king named King Salgyel. He married the daughter of the king of a nearby country, and King Salgyel and his queen were very happy together.

After some time, the queen knew that she was pregnant, and she informed the king. "That is excellent," said King Salgyel. "Whether the child is a boy or a girl, we will love it equally. Whichever God sends us will be a blessing to us."

After the months had passed, the queen began to give birth. She had an easy labor, and her daughter came into the world without difficulty. But when the midwife and the queen looked at the baby, they were horrified because it was the ugliest baby that had ever been seen, uglier than anyone could imagine. The little girl's hair was like a mat of coconut fiber, and her skin was like the bark of a tree. Her face was scrunched up and misshapen; her body was crooked and lame.

Soon the king came into the birth chamber to see his new daughter, and he was horrified, too. But soon he got control of himself and said to his wife, "We cannot escape the karma that has led to this birth, but we must think what to do about what has happened. If we make an announcement of the birth of a daughter, then the kings of other countries will send ambassadors asking that their princes be betrothed to her. Then we would have the terrible embarrassment of explaining to them that our daughter is too ugly to be the wife of a prince. On the other hand, we cannot make an announcement now saying what has really happened. The only thing to do is to make no announcement at all and keep this birth a secret from the world. We will raise this daughter secretly and treat her with kindness and consideration, but she cannot be part of the public life of the royal family."

The queen agreed with this, so they made no announcement at all about the birth of a child. The people of the kingdom were very puzzled by this, and many rumors went around about what might have become of the new royal baby, but the secret was well kept, and none of the people had any true understanding of what had happened.

The king gave orders that a special small house, surrounded by a high fence, should be built within the palace grounds for the little girl, who they named Dorjee. She had one nurse to take care of her, and one of the king's ministers was told the secret so that he could handle anything that might come up concerning the child. King Salgyel and his queen were kind to their child and often visited her in her little house. She was a sweet-tempered and intelligent girl, and she became quite accomplished at weaving and embroidery and other arts suitable to a royal princess, but she never grew one single bit less ugly.

The years passed by, one after another, and soon Princess Dorjee was almost eighteen years old. It was not suitable that a royal princess should remain unmarried beyond the age of eighteen, so it was necessary to find a husband for her; on the other hand, the problem of her appearance made things very difficult.

The king summoned the minister who was in on the secret of Princess Dorjee and said to him, "It is time for the princess to be married. I have been thinking carefully of who her husband should be. Do you know of any family in my kingdom that is of high noble lineage, but now has become very poor? If there is any such family and they have a son of the proper age, he would be a suitable husband for her."

The minister said that he knew of exactly such a family, an old and proud family of noble lineage that now had become very poor. "Their son, Tashi, would be a perfect husband for the princess," said the minister. "And if he is able to marry a daughter of the royal family, his family will be saved from their poverty."

Then the king sent out messengers to bring young Tashi to court. "Young man," said the king, "I have decided that you should marry my daughter, Princess Dorjee. I don't suppose you knew that I have such a daughter."

"I did not know, Your Majesty," said Tashi, "but I am most honored by your commandment. I will be very happy to marry your daughter."

"There is just one thing that you need to know first, although it doesn't change anything," said the king. "But it is only fair to warn you ahead of time: my daughter is hideously ugly. She will be the ugliest person you've ever seen. I don't suppose that she is exactly what you had in mind for a wife."

"That doesn't matter at all," replied Tashi. "I am still honored to marry your daughter. And anyway, I am your loyal subject, and you have given me a command. I would marry your dog if you commanded me to. I am ready to have the wedding whenever you wish."

"Excellent," said the king. And he gave orders for a small wedding feast to be held in secret in the innermost part of the palace.

Again the people of the kingdom were puzzled by this. On the one had, it seemed clear that some sort of wedding feast had been celebrated in the palace, but on the other hand, no announcement of it had been made. Again there were rumors flying about the country, but no one could guess what had really happened.

Even more mysteriously, a young man from a noble but very poor and obscure family was now living in the palace and was being treated as a royal prince. Surely, people said, he must have married a daughter of the king. But, others asked, wouldn't a king's daughter have been sent to marry a prince from another country, rather than such a nobody? People could not figure out what was going on.

The young man's friends began talking among themselves about what had happened to him.

"He surely has married a princess," said one.

"But we don't know if there even is a princess," said another.

"In any case, why would such a marriage be kept secret?" asked a third.

"I know the answer to that," said one of the other friends. "She must be either extremely ugly or extremely beautiful. If she is ugly, she would be an embarrassment to the royal family. If she is beautiful, maybe they would not be able to bear having her leave them to marry a prince in some distant country. In any case, we must follow him to see where he lives within the palace, and then we will be able to make some plan to learn his secret."

The next day, one of the friends (whose father was a minister, so he could visit the palace without making anyone suspicious) followed Prince Tashi until he saw him go to a small house, surrounded by a high fence, in a little-visited part of the palace. The prince carefully unlocked the gate of the fence and put the key into a fold of his robe.

Going back to where his friends were waiting, the minister's son told them all that he had seen. One of them said, "We must find a way to get the key. But how can we do it, if he always keeps it in a fold of his robe?"

"That shouldn't be too hard," said another. "Let's give a party for him and get him drunk. Then we can take the key without him knowing it, and we will see what is inside that little house."

A few nights later, the friends told Prince Tashi that they were giving a party for him and that he had to come as the honored guest. He agreed, and on the night of the party he said goodbye to his wife.

"I'm going out tonight, my dear," he said. "Some friends are giving me a party. I'm sorry to say this, but I'm sure you understand that you will have to stay here alone this evening. I'll probably be back rather late." And so he took his leave.

After he had left the house, Princess Dorjee went over to the small altar of the Buddha that she kept in her house and knelt down to pray.

"Please help me, Lord Buddha," she prayed. "I don't understand why I have to be so ugly that no one can stand to look at me. Why has this happened to me? Also, I am very grateful to have such a good and kind husband, but I wish I could please him more. It must not be easy for him to be married to someone as ugly as me. Isn't there anything I can do?"

Just then, a visualization of the Buddha began to appear before her. At first it was just a tiny, glowing jewel hovering in midair; this was the crown of wisdom at the top of the Buddha's head. As soon as it appeared, Princess Dorjee's old hair, like a matted clump of coconut fiber, was replaced by long, lustrous black hair, silky and shining, hanging down her back.

Then the face of the Buddha appeared, and at the same instant Princess Dorjee's ugly face was replaced by a face of such radiant loveliness that anyone who saw her would instantly fall in love with her. After that the body of the Buddha appeared in the visualization, floating in midair, and Princess Dorjee's lame, crooked body covered with skin like ragged tree bark suddenly

changed into a beautiful body, with round, full breasts, a slender
waist, wide hips, and skin as smooth and pale as newly woven silk.
Her arms were supple and slender, her legs long and shapely, her
feet graceful and small. She was perfectly beautiful in every
respect.

Princess Dorjee was deeply shocked and surprised at the
change that had come over her and a bit frightened, too. "Please,
Lord Buddha," she prayed. "Help me to understand the meaning
of this."

A voice came from the visualization of the Buddha saying,
"This is all the result of karma. I will explain to you what it
means."

So Princess Dorjee listened carefully to the Buddha's teaching and then sat quietly waiting for her husband to return.

MEANWHILE, PRINCE TASHI'S friends made sure that he drank
a great deal of wine at their party. They gave toast after toast, and
he had to empty his glass each time. They played drinking games,
and it seemed that in every game it was he who had to drink a for-
feit cup. Being from a poor but upright family, he was not at all
used to drinking to excess, and it wasn't long before he passed out
from drinking too much. His friends quickly took the key to his
gate out of the folds of his robe and went off to see what his wife
looked like.

Very quietly they unlocked the gate and crept into the little
house, trying to see the prince's wife without her being aware of
their presence. When they looked into her small room, they saw
her sitting in prayer in front of the altar of the Buddha; at their
first glance of her, they were thunderstruck by her beauty. Several
of them nearly fainted, and all of them knew that no woman that

they would ever see for the rest of their lives would be able to compete with the beauty of their friend's wife.

Completely amazed, they crept back out of the room and returned to the party hall, where the prince was still sleeping in a drunken stupor. "Now I understand the sage wisdom of our good King Salgyel," said one of the friends. "His daughter is so extraordinarily beautiful, he realized that if she were allowed to be seen by anyone outside the royal family, all of the kingdoms on the borders of our own country would continually be at war competing for the opportunity to marry one of their princes to her. It was better to shut her up in her own garden than to allow her beauty to disturb the peace of the world forever." All of the friends agreed with this explanation, and they went home full of admiration for the wisdom of their king.

Hours later, just before dawn, Prince Tashi awoke with a terrible hangover to discover that he was alone in the party hall. Feeling rather annoyed with his friends for letting him get so drunk and then leaving him alone, he staggered home. When he had unlocked the gate and entered their little house, he was astonished to see an extraordinarily beautiful young woman sitting there. "Who are you?" he asked. "And where is my wife, Princess Dorjee?"

"Look at me, husband, I am she," said the princess.

"No, that's quite impossible," said the prince. "I'm sorry to say this, but my wife is hideously ugly. You are obviously not her. What have you done with her?"

"Husband, listen to my voice. Listen to the words I am speaking to you from my heart. I am your wife. I am Princess Dorjee. I have been transformed through the grace of the Lord Buddha, but I am still the same person as before. Please do not reject me now, my beloved husband."

"I believe you," said Prince Tashi. "It is very hard to understand what has happened, but I do believe that you are my wife. I am very happy for you that this amazing transformation has taken place. Please may I summon your parents so that they may share this joy also?"

"Yes, husband, please do. I think they will be very pleased."

So the prince went to find King Salgyel, who came at once with the queen to see what had happened because although the prince had explained it to them, they found it hard to believe until they could see it with their own eyes. When they saw how ravishingly beautiful their daughter had become, they were so happy they could not contain themselves and hugged and kissed her over and over again.

"But," said the king, "I don't understand how this amazing transformation came about."

"The Lord Buddha explained it to me by giving me a teaching while the visualization was still before my eyes," said the princess. "And indeed the ugliness that I bore for so many years was entirely my fault. It was the fulfillment of my karma, just as the beauty that now is mine is a release from that karma. This is what I was taught:

"Many lifetimes ago, thousands of years ago, in fact, I was born as the daughter of a very respectable and pious family. My family gave alms to beggars, and food to monks, and part of their wealth to temples, but especially they supported a meditation master who lived in that city. They provided almost all of his support, year after year, and considered it a privilege to support the work of such a holy man.

"I, however, complained to them about the meditation master because he was one of the ugliest men that had ever been seen. He was dark and hairy and misshapen, with a nose like a mango and big hairy ears hanging from the sides of his head, and every other part of his face and body was as ugly as these things I have told you about. I told my parents that I hated to see him come into the house; whenever they fed him at our table, I lost my appetite; whenever they gave money to him, I thought that they were fools for giving to someone who obviously could not find favor with the Lord Buddha.

"One day, the meditation master came to our house and said, 'The time has now come for me to die. But before I depart from this world, I want to show you my soul to remind you that great beauty can be concealed beneath a superficial covering of ugliness.' And he let us see his soul, which stretched out in the air before us in all directions, looking like a beautiful garden filled with lovely green plants and clear pools of water, graceful buildings, and sweet music.

"Then the vision faded, and I said to him, 'Master, I am so sorry for having mocked your ugliness. It was so ignorant and mean of me. Can you forgive me?'

"'I forgive you,' said the master, 'but you will bear this karmic burden for many lifetimes. One day, you too will know what it is to be so ugly that you are shunned by one and all. Do not forget, then, that great beauty can exist beneath a veneer of ugliness.'

"So my birth as a hideously ugly baby was the fulfillment of my karma, and my present beauty is a gift of the Buddha when I prayed for understanding.

"Thank you, my husband, for being kind to me when it must have been difficult for you even to look at me," said Princess Dorjee. "I will do my best to serve you well now that I am beautiful."

After this, the princess, her parents, and her husband shared many happy years together.

The Pig's-Head Seer

"Lord Nagarjuna, I don't think I'll ever succeed in bringing Ngudup Dorjee back to your cave," said Dersang, who was feeling quite miserable.

"Nonsense, my boy," replied the saint. "You just need to perfect your mindfulness and you'll be able to succeed. You mustn't give up. Keep trying, and I think you will succeed sooner or later."

"But he always tells a story while I am carrying him back here in the sack, and I can't help listening," said Dersang. "And when I get caught up in the story, I just can't keep my mouth shut."

"Then here is your chance to try again," replied Nagarjuna. "Here is a container of food for your journey, here is a new bag and leather strap, and here is the axe. Try to bring Ngudup Dorjee all the way back to the cave this time."

As he was walking to the old cemetery, Dersang kept repeating to himself, "I will not say a word, I will not say a word, I will not . . ." And soon he was at the cemetery gate. Ignoring all of the other spirits who pretended to be Ngudup Dorjee, he chased the real Ngudup Dorjee up a tree and got out his axe.

"I will cut down this tree at once if you don't come down by yourself," said Dersang.

"Don't bother, boy," said Ngudup Dorjee. "I'm coming

down. You've caught me again. In fact, I'm looking forward to the walk back to your master's cave. I have a very good story to tell you." And he didn't resist at all when Dersang stuffed him into the bag and threw the bag over his shoulder.

As he found the path back home through the woods again, Dersang kept repeating to himself, "I will not say a word, I will not say a word."

"Are you ready, boy?" said Ngudup Dorjee. "This is how my story begins."

ONCE UPON a time, in a certain place, there lived a married couple. They were very much in love and very happy with each other, but they were also as different from one another as they could be. The wife, Yangzom, was full of energy and was always working— cooking, cleaning, working in the garden, taking care of the animals, and doing a dozen other tasks at once. On the other hand, the husband, Pelgay, was extremely lazy. Never mind helping with the cooking and cleaning; he wouldn't do anything at all. He couldn't even be bothered to get dressed properly because putting on his clothes seemed like too much work, so he just covered his body with a length of old cloth. Every day Pelgay would sit in a chair, or lie in bed, or if the sun was nice and warm, he would sprawl on the front steps of their house. Yangzom often urged him to get out and do something, but he was too lazy to take her advice. But she was very kind and always took good care of him and always forgave him for being lazy.

One day, however, even he was bored with being lazy and doing nothing, so he walked out a few steps in front of their house before he sat down to rest. Just then, a crow flew overhead, carrying a half-full butter bag that had fallen from the pack of a butter-merchant's yak. The crow was having a hard time carrying such a heavy thing, and just as it flew overhead it dropped the bag, which landed right in front of the husband.

Pelgay was amazed at his good luck. He picked up the bag, turned it this way and that, and looked it over. Then he opened the bag and saw that it contained a lot of good-quality butter that he and Yangzom could put in their tea, or use to make barley-butter balls, or use to fill the butter lamps in their household shrine.

"Look, dear, what a crow dropped right in front of me," said Pelgay, bringing the bag inside to show to his wife. "It's a half-full bag of good butter."

"Haven't I always told you that good things would happen if you would only get out of the house sometimes?" said Yangzom. "The world is full of people coming and going, and doing this and that, and if you get involved in that, sometimes interesting things will happen."

"Now I feel like going out more myself," said Pelgay. "In fact, tomorrow I will go on a long journey. Maybe something interesting will happen that will make our fortune."

"That's excellent," said Yangzom. "What do you need for the journey?"

"I plan to go far," said Pelgay, "so I need a horse. And naturally I need a saddle, and bridle, and reins, and a lead rope for the horse. Also I want a dog to go along with me for companionship and protection. And finally, I need a wide-brimmed hat to keep the sun from my face."

"That's all fine," said Yangzom. "I can get you all of those things. I'll have them ready for you in the morning."

The next morning, Pelgay mounted the horse, put on his hat, and accompanied by the dog, he rode off into the distance.

He rode up across a mountain pass and down into a deserted valley. As he was riding along, suddenly a fox ran right across the path in front of him. Immediately his dog started to chase the fox, and Pelgay on his horse came riding along behind the dog, but soon the fox ran into a hole in the ground where it had a den, and so it escaped.

Looking around, Pelgay saw that there were actually two holes in the ground, close together. "This is a clever fox," he thought. "If I try to dig it out from one hole, it will run out the other hole and escape. Surely a fox knows its own den, and this fox has made sure it has an escape hole to keep it out of danger. But I have a plan that the fox doesn't know about."

He tied the horse's lead rope to the dog's leash so that neither one would wander away. Then he took off his hat and put it over one of the entrance holes to the fox's den. "This way, when the fox tries to get out from the hole, he will see that the entrance is covered up," he thought. "The fox will become confused, and I will be able to catch it. Fox skins are worth a lot of money, so my wife will be very pleased about this."

Because the day had grown warm, Pelgay took off his heavy sheepskin coat and tied it across his horse's saddle. Then he began to dig at one of the entrance holes to the fox's den. But the fox, in a panic, ran out the other hole without noticing whether it was blocked up or not. The hat stuck right on top of the fox's head, and the fox, wearing the hat, took off across the valley as fast as it could run.

Seeing the fox running away, the dog immediately started chasing it. And because the dog's leash was tied to the horse's lead rope, the horse had to come running along behind the dog. Soon the fox, the dog, and the horse had run completely out of sight, and Pelgay was left standing by the empty fox's den, with no horse, no dog, no coat, and no hat. "This is very bad luck," he thought. "I'd better find my way out of this empty valley."

He walked for many, many miles, up another mountain, across a high pass, and down to another valley, where he found a small kingdom. He walked into the kingdom's main town, but by then the weather had become terrible; it was dark and cold and raining, and all of the streets of the town were deserted, as people stayed inside their houses to keep warm and dry. Anyway Pelgay had no money with him because everything he had was in the saddle-bags of his horse, so he couldn't afford to stay even in the smallest and cheapest inn in the town. After awhile he found a stable full of cattle and yaks, and outside the stable door was a haystack. Tired, cold, hungry, and miserable, he crawled inside the haystack and went to sleep.

Pelgay woke up at dawn and crawled out of his hiding place in the haystack. The rain had stopped, and it was a bright, sunny day. Because he had no money for food and no place to go and nothing to do, he sat down by the side of a plaza near the center of town. He was a strange sight, with his dirty clothes and bits of hay sticking to his clothing and in his hair; many people looked at him, but no one spoke to him or challenged him. So he just sat and watched the people walking to and fro. He especially enjoyed watching a group of young girls having fun together, running around and laughing as they played one game after another. As he was watching, he saw that the turquoise stone that one of the girls was wearing on her neck fell to the ground because the string that was holding it around her neck broke. She didn't seem to notice because she was playing so intently, and he felt shy about calling out to her to tell her what had happened.

After awhile the girls went away, and the traveler saw the turquoise stone still lying on the ground. He felt worried because he knew that this was not just an ordinary piece of jewelry; it was the girl's sacred turquoise, which contained part of her soul. If she did not get the stone back, her life would be in danger. So he watched where the stone lay on the ground, thinking to himself, "I should pick it up and find the girl and give it back to her." But he realized that he had no idea where the girl had gone and he had no way of finding her. Then he thought, "I should pick it up anyway, at least. But if I pick it up and do not give it back to her, how am I different from an ordinary thief? What should I do?"

As Pelgay was thinking, a small herd of cows began to walk through the plaza. Just as they came to where the girl's sacred turquoise was lying on the ground, one of the cows began to drop dung, as cows often do, and as it walked along it dropped one big, wet cow turd right on top of the turquoise. Pelgay watched this and made a careful mental note of which turd hid the turquoise, thinking that when the cows had walked away, he could go and pick up the cow turd and find the turquoise again.

But just then, an old woman came along with a wooden scoop to collect the cow turds to dry and use for fuel. She picked up turd after turd and flung them against the wall of a nearby house, where they could dry out enough to burn. Pelgay watched carefully as she picked up the turd with the turquoise and flung it against the wall; he memorized the pattern of the dung on the wall so that he would remember exactly which one contained the turquoise.

He was just about to walk over and pry the right lump of dung off the wall when the plaza began to get very crowded with people. He walked closer to where the people were crowding around and saw that a large piece of paper was glued to the wall of one of the houses there. He couldn't read, of course, because he had always been too lazy to learn, but he asked one of the people standing there what the paper said. "It says that the king's daughter has lost her sacred turquoise," the bystander said. "The king is offering a big reward to anyone who can find it. If the person who finds it is a man, the king will make him his prime minister, and if it is a woman, the king will grant her rank equal to that of the queen."

At the royal palace, the princess was growing more and more weak from the loss of part of her soul. Her doctors were very worried about her. Meanwhile, in the throne room the king and all of his ministers were talking about the crisis. One of the king's ministers mentioned a report that a badly dressed stranger had been seen in the city. "Maybe we should bring him to the palace to see if he can help us find the turquoise," said the minister. "Sometimes strangers have unusual powers that we locals know nothing about." So the king ordered the stranger to be brought to the palace at once.

"Stranger," said the king, "we urgently need to find the princess's lost turquoise. Do you have any special powers that could help us to search for it?"

The traveler of course knew exactly where the turquoise was, so he said to the king, "Your Majesty, it happens that I do have a special skill that will enable me to find your daughter's sacred turquoise. But you must agree to provide me with everything I need for my work."

"What do you need?" asked the king.

"I need the head of a freshly killed pig," said Pelgay, "mounted on the end of a long stick and tied on securely with a length of the pig's intestine."

"That will be very easy to provide," said the king. "Do you need anything else?"

"No, that will be sufficient," said Pelgay. So the king ordered that the pig's-head staff should be prepared at once and brought to the stranger at the palace.

When it was ready, Pelgay led the king and all the ministers back to the plaza downtown, where he began to point the pig's-head staff at one person after another. As he did so, he said in a powerful, deep, chanting voice, like the voice of a lama, "Is it here? No, not here. Maybe over there? No, not there either.

Maybe here?" He chanted and pointed the staff at one person after another, and then changed his chant, "No, not with people, maybe somewhere else. Maybe in this doorway, no not here, maybe on this wall . . ." And pointing the staff exactly at the lump of dung that he knew contained the turquoise, he chanted, "Maybe here, maybe here . . . yes! Right here!" And he ordered one of the king's servants to pull the lump of dung down from the wall. And right inside it, to everyone's amazement, was the princess's turquoise.

The king, keeping his promise, offered to make Pelgay his new prime minister, but Pelgay replied, "No, thank you, Your Majesty. I have no experience of being prime minister, and I think I would not be very good at it. I don't want to disappoint you. I just will ask you for a small reward, and then I will go back to my home."

"What reward do you want?" asked the king.

"When I was on my way to your kingdom, I lost everything I had," he replied. "So I would like to have a fox, and a horse with a saddle and bridle and reins, and a dog with a leash, and a good hat with a wide brim. Fox pelts are worth a lot of money," he added.

"It will be very easy for us to give you all of those things," said the king, "but are you sure that's enough?"

"That really is fine, Your Majesty. Thank you very much."

"Then you shall have everything you asked for, and I will also give you a new title, by royal command. From now on, your name is the Pig's-Head Seer."

Pelgay was delighted with all of this so he took his reward and went back home. When he arrived, Yangzom said to him, "Husband, I'm so glad you're back. You've been gone for quite a few days now. I was beginning to worry that you were gone forever. Sit down and tell me everything that's happened."

So Pelgay told his wife the whole story from beginning to

end. "That was a wonderful adventure," she said. "Didn't I tell you that interesting things would happen if you would just leave the house once in awhile? There's only one trouble, and that is you did not ask for a big enough reward. After all, you saved the princess's life."

Then Yangzom sat down and wrote a letter to the king, explaining that her husband had gotten confused in all of the excitement after he had saved the princess's life and he did not think to ask for a big enough reward. Would the king please send some other things that would be more suitable than just a fox, a horse, a dog, and a hat?

When the king received the letter, he was very pleased because he had worried that it was not honorable for him to have let the stranger go without a big enough reward. So he sent many yaks loaded down with treasures to the house of the Pig's-Head Seer and his wife. In that way they became very rich, and they enjoyed a happy life together.

But meanwhile the reputation of the Pig's-Head Seer as someone who could find even the most deeply hidden secrets continued to spread. The Pig's-Head Seer didn't realize it, but something that was happening in a small kingdom far away was about to cause trouble for him.

That small kingdom was ruled by a very wise and good king who had seven sons. The kingdom was very prosperous and happy because the king was wise and good, and the princes were all fine young men who loved and supported one another without any trace of jealousy. So all of the people in the kingdom could go about their business without worrying about their government being weak or cruel.

But just in the next valley, beyond that kingdom, was another kingdom, not of humans but of *sinpo* shape-shifting monsters who liked to catch humans whenever they could and feed on their flesh. So the king and his seven princes always had to be on guard to prevent an invasion from the kingdom of the shape-shifters, and so far they had always managed to keep their kingdom safe.

The *sinpo* were terrible monsters, ugly and cruel. The men were hairy and dark, with fangs and bulging eyes; their skin was covered with warts, and their hands and feet were like bear's paws. The women were just as bad, with long, stringy hair; sharp teeth; big, flat noses; and breasts that sagged down so far on their chests that they could throw them over their shoulders. But the dangerous thing about the *sinpo* is that they were shape-shifters, able to transform themselves into any kind of animal, or even to make themselves look like handsome or beautiful human beings.

One day, the prince of the shape-shifters said to his sister, "Sister, how are we going to defeat the kingdom in the next valley so we can feed upon the people there and take over their land? We have tried over and over to defeat them in battle, but their defenses are too strong."

"Brother," she replied, "we should not try to defeat them in battle, but rather we should destroy them from within. If you will change yourself into a fine, big yak, I will show you what to do next."

So the shape-shifter prince transformed himself into a fine, big yak, and his sister then transformed herself into a beautiful young woman. Piling the yak's saddle-bags full of gold and silk and other treasures, she set off along the road to the neighboring kingdom. When she got there, she went straight to the main city market and began buying and selling with the other merchants there, unloading one kind of wonderful object after another from the saddle-bags of her handsome, big yak.

Of course, the rumor of this beautiful young woman doing business in the market soon spread throughout the city, and it

reached the ears of the oldest of the seven princes. He went down
to the market to see what was going on, and as soon as he saw the
young woman, he fell in love with her. "If only I could marry this
beautiful young woman, I know I would be happy forever," he
thought. He sent a servant to run back to the palace to tell his six
brothers, and they all came down to the market as well. And all
of them immediately also fell in love with the young woman.

In many places this might have caused a problem, but the
seven brothers were never jealous of one another, and anyway this
was in Tibet, where it is common for several brothers to all marry
one single wife. So the brothers said to each other, "This is not a
problem. We will all marry this beautiful young girl, and we will
all be equally her husbands. Let's tell our father about this now."

When they told the king, he was pleased at the news, but
he did not want to give his approval until he had met the young
woman himself. So he sent servants to invite her to the palace.
When she had arrived, he asked, "Who are you, may I ask, and
how do you happen to be in my kingdom?"

"I am Princess Palmo from a kingdom east of India," she
replied, "but I became bored with the dull life in the palace, so I
have disguised myself as an ordinary market woman, and I have
been traveling here and there, exchanging one kind of merchandise
for another wherever the road might take me."

"This is very good," thought the king. "She is certainly of
royal birth and of high enough rank to marry my sons. Further-
more she is very beautiful, and they are all very much in love with
her. Now I can retire from being king. All seven of my sons will
become the husbands of this beautiful Princess Palmo, and my
oldest son will become king in my place."

Things happened exactly as the old king commanded. The
seven sons became the husbands of Princess Palmo, the old king
retired to a quiet home in the countryside, and the oldest prince

became king in his place. The husbands and the bride seemed very happy together, and the only thing that anyone found strange is that the young queen always seemed to like to have her favorite yak with her.

Everything was fine for a few months, but then the young king fell ill. He had pains in his chest and could hardly breathe, and he felt his soul becoming weaker and weaker. He knew that he would die soon, no matter what his doctors might do. And that is what happened; the king's doctors tried medicine and chanting and exorcism and everything else they could think of, but nothing worked, and soon the king was dead.

The next oldest prince became king then, and for a few months everything was fine. But then he, too, fell ill, with pain and weakness and no breath and a sickness in his soul; he knew that no matter what the doctors might do, he would die soon. And that is what happened; he died in spite of everything that the doctors tried, and the next brother became king in his place.

That king died, too, and the next king, and the next, until only the youngest prince was left, and he became king in his turn. All of the ministers, and all of the people in the kingdom, were growing frantic with worry. The high ministers of the kingdom got together, and the prime minister said, "This is the most terrible crisis that any of us have ever experienced. We are down to our last king. If he also falls ill and dies, there will be no one to lead the defense against the kingdom of the shape-shifters in the next valley. Our kingdom will be lost, and we will all die horribly."

Another minister said, "Let's send messengers to other countries, far and wide, and see if anyone in some other kingdom can help us find out why our kings are dying and help us to save our kingdom."

The ministers agreed that this was a good idea, so messengers were sent in all directions to try to find a way to keep the last king from falling ill and dying. And that is how a messenger showed up at the door of the great Pig's-Head Seer one morning.

"Your honor," said the messenger to him, "your reputation has spread everywhere, and as soon as I heard about you I rode to your door. Everyone knows that there is no one in the world better than you at finding secrets that are hidden. Please come to my kingdom to find out why our kings have been dying and to help save our youngest king. If you succeed, the king will reward you with any riches you want."

"Wait a moment," said the Pig's-Head Seer, and he went in to talk with his wife. "This is terrible," he said to Yangzom. "You and I know that I really don't have any special powers at all. I was able to find the princess's sacred turquoise because I knew exactly where it was. It really was a sort of a trick. But I have no idea why these kings have been dying. I think I must refuse to go with this messenger."

"If you go and do not succeed," said Yangzom, "no one will blame you. They will just say that the magic that has been killing the kings is too strong for you. But if you refuse to go, it is as much as admitting that you have no special powers, and your reputation is a fraud. I think you really must go. You have nothing to lose, and who knows? Maybe you will think of something when you get there."

Just as his wife advised, the Pig's-Head Seer told the messenger that he would be ready to leave as soon as his horse was saddled. He said goodbye to Yangzom and rode off to the distant kingdom.

When the seer and the messenger arrived, they found that their worst fears had come true. The young king had fallen ill while the messenger was gone and was now on the verge of death. "You must come and see him right away," the prime minister said to the seer. "Only you can save him."

The Pig's-Head Seer was shown into the royal bedchamber, where the young king, pale and exhausted, was lying in bed. When he heard that the seer had arrived, however, he sat up with a smile on his face and said, "Welcome! We have been waiting for you for many weeks. I'm sure that things will get better now that you are here to discover why my brothers died and why I am so ill also. Actually, I already feel much better just knowing that you are here." Having said that, the king really did look somewhat better. Some rosy color returned to his cheeks, and his breathing became easier; he sat up and began chatting with his ministers about his plans for after he got well again.

But the Pig's-Head Seer was very troubled by what he saw because he was afraid the king was experiencing the kind of false recovery that sometimes occurs just a few hours before death. "The king is not going to get better," he thought. "He will be dead before daylight."

The seer was given a good dinner, and the prime minister personally showed him to a comfortable bedroom in the palace. "Rest now," he said, "and in the morning you can use your skill to find out why these misfortunes have plagued our kingdom."

Alone in his room, the seer was feeling miserable. "Why did I come here?" he said to himself. "The king will be dead soon, and there's nothing I can do to change that. I have no skills; I'm just a fraud. It was a mistake to come here. I will run away back home tonight."

Late that night, he opened his window and climbed down the wall of the palace. When he got down, he found himself in a stable yard so he went to the royal stables to try to find his horse. But when he went inside, all of the king's horses began to stamp their feet and whinny. He was afraid that the horses would wake the guards, so he went outside again. Then he tried another building, but it was full of sheep and goats, and they were of no use to him. Then he tried a third building, and when he stepped inside, he immediately ran into something large and soft, which made him trip and fall on his face. He saw that it was a large yak lying right by the door. He became so angry at the yak for tripping him that he picked up a stick and began to beat the yak very severely. And as he was doing so, he felt someone, or something, rush past him, and he heard the door open and then slam closed again.

Frightened, the seer stopped beating the yak and hurried further into the building, where he decided to hide until he was sure it was safe to come out again. Soon afterward, he heard the door open again, and then he was aware that someone had come in and was standing next to the yak. He crept forward to see what was happening and almost let out a scream when he saw, not a yak, but a terrible male *sinpo* shape-shifter demon with hairy skin covered with warts and with bulging eyes and dripping fangs, who was talking with a female *sinpo* with stringy hair and a big, flat nose, sharp teeth, ugly skin, and long pendulous breasts flung over her shoulders. "What happened?" the female asked.

"Some unknown person came into the barn and began beating me," said the male *sinpo*. "I'm afraid it must have been this Pig's-Head Seer we've been hearing about, and that he has discovered our secret. Why else would he beat me so severely for no reason?"

"That's not true," said the female. "I've seen this so-called seer at the palace, and I can tell you that he knows nothing at all. He's just an ignorant country person; we don't need to be afraid of him. Keep your courage up. Tomorrow the young king will surely die, and we can take over his kingdom. Go back to sleep now. I have to get back to the palace." And she immediately changed herself into the beautiful Queen Palmo and hurried back to the palace without anyone seeing her.

The seer waited a long time for the male demon, who had

changed himself back into a yak, to fall asleep. Then he crept out
of the stable building and went back to his room in the palace.

The same morning, at dawn, he sent word to all of the ministers to meet him in the king's bedchamber. When they had all
arrived, he said to the king, "Your Majesty, I already know what
killed all of your brothers and what is making you ill. But I am
quite sure that the answer will not please you at all. In fact, I'm
afraid that when I tell you the answer, you will punish me instead
of giving me a reward because I will tell you something that you
would rather not know."

"No," said the king, "that can't be true. Whatever you tell
me, I will thank you for it. We all are counting on your help. If
you fail, I will die and my kingdom will be lost. Tell me now, what
have you found out?"

"I can't tell you now, Your Majesty," said the seer, "but I will
tell you tomorrow after certain preparations have been made. First
you must issue orders to the peasants to go into the forest and cut
down all of the trees, and pile the wood in the middle of the
parade grounds to prepare a big bonfire. And then you must order
that every person in the whole kingdom must come to the parade
grounds tomorrow morning to witness what will happen there,
and that anyone who is absent will be punished."

"Those things are easily done," said the king, and he sent one
of his ministers out to write a proclamation that would be read in
every town and village and farm in the kingdom. For the rest of
the day, one could hear sounds in the distance of trees being cut
down and wood being piled high in the center of the parade
grounds, but the seer refused to say anything more about what he
had in mind.

The next day, the king was carried in a sedan chair to the
parade grounds. Arriving there, he rested on a high reviewing
stand surrounded by all of his ministers. In the center of the
parade grounds, a towering bonfire had been prepared and around

it were thousands and thousands of people—the entire population of the kingdom.

"Are you ready, Seer?" shouted the prime minister.

"Ready, Your Excellency," replied the seer. "Light the bonfire. And guards, seize that yak! Tie it up tightly so it cannot escape."

Walking over to where the yak was lying on its side, securely bound with ropes, the seer said to it, "Monster, you have one chance and one chance only. Tell me how you and your sister have been plotting to take over this kingdom, or I will have you thrown into the bonfire at once."

The *sinpo* knew that there was no other way to save his life so, still in the shape of the yak, he began to speak. "Yes, it's true, we did kill all of the kings one after another, and we will kill this young king, too. But it was not my fault; it was all my sister's idea. She is the one who is behind it all."

"And who is your sister?" asked the Pig's-Head Seer. "Show us now."

"It is her, Queen Palmo," shouted the yak. "Please spare my life; it was all her fault."

"Guards! Seize the queen," shouted the seer. "Tie her up. Don't let her escape." When Queen Palmo was lying tied up next to the yak, the seer said to her, "Confess! Tell your husband how you murdered his brothers and were planning to murder him."

"Yes, it is true," said the queen. "And it would have worked if it had not been for you, you miserable country bumpkin of a seer. How did you find out about us anyway?"

And with that, both the queen and the yak transformed back into *sinpo* demons, and they were so ugly and horrible that most of the people could not even bear to look at them. But the brave guards picked them up and hurled them into the bonfire, and they were burned to a crisp.

The king's health recovered immediately when false Queen

Palmo had burned to death, so he knew for sure that the Pig's-Head Seer had been right about everything. "Thank you so much, Seer," said the king. "Now all that remains is for you to name your reward."

"What I really want is just to go home," said the seer. "But my wife was saying just the other day that she needs a new loom. Perhaps you could give me a good one, and that would be my reward."

"Nonsense!" cried the old retired king, who had been listening to all of this from his place in the crowd. "You have saved my son's life, and you have saved our whole kingdom, and you surely will have a greater reward than a new loom. I insist that you and your wife move here to this kingdom, and you will be my guests in my country estate for the rest of your lives. And anything you ask for will be yours."

So the seer sent for Yangzom, and they both lived in the old king's country estate for the rest of their lives, which were long and happy ones. And the young king married a very suitable princess and ruled his country well for a very long time.

"WOW! THAT Pig's-Head Seer was really good at finding things out," said Dersang. As the strap broke and the bag burst open, Ngudup Dorjee gave Dersang a sharp slap on the cheek as a reminder to keep his mouth shut. "Goodbye, boy," laughed Ngudup Dorjee as he flew back to the old cemetery. "I'll expect to see you again soon."

Langa and Jatsalu

"Goodbye, Lord Nagarjuna," called Dersang. "I'm off to the old cemetery. I really think I'll succeed this time."

"I hope so," said the saint. "And I'm glad you're feeling confident. Just be sure you're not fooling yourself."

"I know," said Dersang. "I'll see you soon." He put his food container in his shoulder-bag, draped a new sack and leather strap over his shoulder, picked up the old axe, and set off.

When he got to the old cemetery, Dersang called out as usual. "Ngudup Dorjee, where are you? Where is Ngudup Dorjee?" Ngudup Dorjee hardly made more than a token show of trying to get away. As soon as Dersang came to the tree that he had climbed, Ngudup Dorjee climbed down again and didn't resist at all when Dersang tied him into the sack.

"You know, boy," said Ngudup Dorjee as they started back toward Nagarjuna's cave, "I think it is very inconsiderate of you not to tell me a story for a change. We've made this trip who knows how many times now, and I do all the work. I think it's your turn."

Dersang, of course, said nothing.

"Well, if you won't, I'll have to," sighed Ngudup Dorjee. "But I still think it's not fair. Anyway, see how you like this one."

ONCE UPON a time, in a small valley, there lived a family: a father, a mother, and two beautiful daughters. They made their living by herding sheep, and because they were honest and hardworking, they had many hundreds of sheep and were prosperous and happy.

One day, the father went down to the valley meadow where the sheep were grazing to make sure that everything was all right. But when he reached the valley, he met a terrifying *sinpo* shapeshifter, who seized him in its powerful hands, killed him, skinned him, and ate him. Then the shape-shifter killed and butchered a sheep and put the meat into a leather bag; finally it put on the father's old skin and, looking exactly like the father himself, walked back up the path to the family's home.

"Here is some meat for our supper," he said to his wife, "and I heard some wonderful news today. A king who rules a small kingdom over the mountain has proclaimed that he is searching for a pure and beautiful young woman to be his wife. I'm sure our eldest daughter would do very well."

The wife thought that was a wonderful idea, so after supper she got out the daughter's best clothing and her own finest jewelry to be ready to send the daughter off in the morning. And when morning came, the mother helped her daughter to dress and put on the jewelry and to arrange her hair, and she thought that no other girl could possibly be as beautiful.

The false father walked with the daughter on the path through the sheep meadow that would lead to the pass over the mountain, but no sooner were they out of sight of the house than the shape-shifter killed the daughter and ate her. Then he waited until almost nightfall, when he killed and butchered a sheep and brought the meat to the family's house again.

"Excellent news," he said to the wife. "The king accepted our daughter to be his bride. Not only that, but he was so pleased with her that he told me his brother was also looking for a bride. I'm sure our younger daughter would do very well."

The younger daughter, whose name was Langa, heard this news but was not altogether pleased by it. She thought that she was still too young to leave home, and also she didn't like the idea of her parents being left all alone with no one to help take care of the house. So she tried to get her mother to refuse to agree to the plan, but her mother thought it would be wonderful for Langa to be married to the brother of the king. So she prepared Langa's best clothing and the rest of the family jewelry to get ready for the morning.

In the morning, the mother helped Langa dress and do her hair and put on the jewelry, and she thought her daughter looked as beautiful as any girl in the kingdom. Then Langa and the false father set out to walk across the mountain pass.

When they reached the meadow, the shape-shifter saw that there were other people on the path, so he wanted to wait until they went away. "Wait here," he said to Langa, showing her where to sit on a stone by the side of the path. "I'll be back soon."

As she was waiting, Langa saw that a small white dog was trotting toward her, wagging its tail. It was a very cute and friendly dog, and she reached down to pet it. "Langa," said the dog (and she was surprised that it could speak and that it knew her name), "I am very hungry. If you give me one piece of bread, I will tell you one secret. If you give me two pieces of bread, I will tell you two secrets. If you give me three pieces of bread, I will tell you three secrets."

Langa had brought food for the journey in her shoulder-bag, but she felt too excited to be hungry so she took out the food and gave it to the dog. "You can have it all," she said.

When the dog had finished eating, it said, "Here is the first secret. The man who seems to be your father is not your father; he is a shape-shifter who has taken on your father's appearance.

"The second secret is that the shape-shifter has killed and eaten both your father and your elder sister. I know that is hard to believe, but if you will follow me, I will show you that it is true." And the dog ran off toward a nearby cave. Langa followed it into the cave and saw the bones of her father and older sister lying there, with some of their clothing and other things that she recognized.

"The third secret is that you must run away or the shape-shifter will kill you and eat you, too. But when you try to run away, the shape-shifter, who is much faster and stronger than you, will follow you and catch you again. Therefore, when you run away, you must be sure to take this plate with you," he said, pointing to a porcelain plate lying on the floor of the cave. "When he grabs hold of you, throw the plate on its rim so that it will roll down the slope of the hill. Then say to the shape-shifter, 'You have caught me, but let me just run after my plate and get it back before you kill me.' When you follow the plate, you will find a way to save yourself." And with that, the dog went trotting away again.

Langa picked up the porcelain plate and began to run away from the cave. But the shape-shifter saw her and ran after her; he soon caught up with her and seized her by the shoulder. Langa threw the plate on its rim, as the dog had told her to do, and it began to roll quickly down the hill. "Yes, you have caught me," said Langa, "but before you kill me, let me just get back my plate that is rolling away down the hill." The shape-shifter let her go, knowing that he could always catch her again, and she ran quickly down the hill after the plate.

The hill got steeper and steeper. The plate rolled faster and faster, and Langa ran after it as fast as she could. In the distance she saw that there was a burlap sack lying on the ground that had been used to carry cow dung. It was very stained and dirty. To her surprise, the plate rolled right into the sack. Coming up to the place where this happened, she picked up the sack and saw that it had concealed a pair of old wooden doors set into the ground. She opened the doors and saw a flight of steps leading down into the ground. She walked down the steps and saw in front of her a big iron door. When she pushed against the door it opened easily, and she saw that there was a corridor beyond the door. Walking farther, she saw a big golden door in front of her, and she pushed that open. too. Then she saw that she was in a room decorated with gold and gemstones. There was a short flight of stairs leading up to a throne on a raised dais, but she couldn't see anyone in the room.

"Welcome to my room," said a low, booming voice. "You must be tired."

"No, I'm not tired. Everything is fine," said Langa, looking around to see where the voice was coming from. Then she noticed that there was a large rooster perched on the banister of the stairs leading up to the throne, and she realized that the rooster was talking to her.

"Are you hungry?" asked the rooster. "There is a kitchen through that door, where you will find plenty of good food." And by this time she was hungry, so she went into the kitchen and ate the delicious meal that she found laid out on the table for her. Then she went back into the main room.

"Are you cold?" asked the rooster. "Through that door is a · bedroom, with plenty of warm clothes in the wooden chests and plenty of blankets for the bed. When you get tired you can sleep there. Tomorrow when you leave here, do not go back out through the corridor; use the small door that is set into the bedroom wall."

It was chilly in the underground house, so Langa went into the bedroom and put on warm clothes. Then she found that she was very tired after all, so she lay down on the bed, covered herself with warm blankets, and fell fast asleep.

In the morning she woke up and found some food waiting for her in the kitchen. When she had finished breakfast, she went back to the bedroom, opened the small door in the wall, and stepped out into the world. She was very surprised to find herself in a crowded marketplace in a city she had never been in before. There were people from many different lands, buying and selling, and there were all sorts of interesting things to look at. She noticed that there were a great many beautiful girls there, but not very many boys.

Meanwhile, back at the house, the rooster took off its rooster skin and out stepped a very handsome young man. He was dressed in very handsome clothing, and he went through another door into a stable, where he placed a fine silver-mounted saddle on a beautiful big horse. Mounting the horse, he rode away to the marketplace in the city.

When he arrived there, all of the people, and especially the pretty girls, crowded around him, crying out, "Jatsalu, Jatsalu, look over here. Come and talk with me, Jatsalu." Jatsalu—for that was the young man's name—rode through the market smiling at people and giving a friendly greeting here and there, but not stopping anywhere. Though he did not give any sign of recognition, he saw Langa in the distance, and she saw him also. Immediately, she fell deeply in love with him and felt that her karma and his had been joined a long time ago.

After awhile, Jatsalu began to ride away from the market, but all of the people still crowded around and followed him. But before he had left his house, he had prepared two sacks that he tied to his saddle-horn. One contained dust and ashes, and the other contained broken pieces of brown sugar. Now, because the people would not stop following him, he emptied the bag of dust and ashes on the road behind him. Many people got dust in their eyes and could not see where they were going, and so they stopped following him. Then, because there were still many people following him, he emptied the bag of brown sugar lumps onto the road behind him, and many people stopped to pick up the sugar lumps and eat them like candy. So no more people were following him after that, and Jatsalu rode home.

Later, Langa also returned to the underground house. When she got there, the rooster said to her, "Did you have an interesting time today?"

"Yes," she said, "there was a big market, and I stayed there all day."

"Were there very many pretty girls there?"

"Yes," said Langa, "many pretty girls, but very few boys."

"You should go again tomorrow," said the rooster.

That night Langa went to sleep in the bedroom again, but in the morning she only pretended to go out of the house to the market town. She opened the little door in the bedroom wall and then, without going out, closed it loudly again. Then she hid behind the clothes in the bedroom, from where she could see through a crack in the door to the throne room.

As she watched, she saw the rooster split open its skin, and out stepped the handsome young man she had seen riding in the market. She waited for him to go out to the stable to get his horse and then stepped quickly into the main room. She made a fire on the hearth, picked up the rooster skin, and threw it into the fire, where it burned up without leaving a trace behind.

That day, when Jatsalu arrived at the market, he looked everywhere for Langa but couldn't find her. He rode his horse around the market square, first clockwise, then counterclockwise, but he didn't see her anywhere. Worried that something might be wrong, he hurried back home. When he reached the house, he immediately sensed that something was wrong. "Who's here?" he shouted. "What's going on?"

"I am here," said Langa, stepping into the room. "And I know that your name is Jatsalu, and I am in love with you."

"But what happened to my rooster skin?" asked Jatsalu, looking very worried.

"I burned it up in the fire," she replied, "because I could not stand to have you disguise yourself from me anymore."

"Oh, my love, that was a terrible mistake," said Jatsalu. "If I still had that rooster skin, it would have been possible for us to be happy together for years to come, but without it I'm afraid our karma together is finished. That disguise was the only thing saving me from my enemies. I had escaped from them, but without that disguise my life will become very difficult and dangerous, and there is no way for you to share it. If you leave here, we still can hope for the future. But for now, we will only have this one night together, and then you must leave here forever."

Langa was horrified to hear that, and she wept and begged Jatsalu's forgiveness. But what was done was done, and there was no way for them to change it. So they spent the night together, sharing their love, and the next day she had to leave forever.

"When you leave the house, walk to the east," Jatsalu told her. "After you have crossed several passes, you will come to my parents' house. It is a big house, with a big family and many servants and many sheep and yaks. Guarding the house are many fierce dogs. They are unlike ordinary dogs because they can understand your motivation. If you show them an attitude of compassion and undivided mind, they will allow you to pass, but if your mind is troubled and full of negative energy, they will bark and growl and attack you, and you will be severely mauled. Do not lose your mindfulness."

With that advice in mind, she left the house, and after walking for many days she reached the home of Jatsalu's parents. Because her mind was concentrated and filled with compassion, the guard dogs didn't bark at her, and they allowed her to pass. Seeing a beautiful young woman standing in the courtyard and realizing that she must be someone special because the dogs did not bother her, Jatsalu's mother invited Langa to come inside.

When she had drunk some tea and rested a bit, Langa sat with Jatsalu's mother and suddenly heaved a big sigh. From that, Jatsalu's mother understood that the young woman was troubled and she asked what was the matter.

"I have a boyfriend," said the girl, "and he is a perfect boyfriend for me, but our karma is at an end, and I am afraid I will never see him again."

Jatsalu's mother answered, "The trouble that you feel is shared by all humanity. Everyone suffers; to live is to suffer. I, too, have suffered a lot. We have lost our son. One day he disappeared, and now we don't know where he is, or whether he is dead or alive." Then the mother said, "You seem to be a well-brought-up young woman, and I feel sorry for your suffering. If you'd like, you can stay here and be one of our servants."

Langa was very upset when she heard the mother talk about how her son had disappeared, but she didn't say anything about that. She just thanked Jatsalu's mother for her kindness and went to find where she should sleep in the servants' quarters.

That night, the little white dog that had saved Langa's life in the sheep meadow came to her in a dream and said, "Soon you will meet a *dransong* truth-sayer holy man. He will help you. Pay careful attention to what he tells you to do." Then Langa woke up.

Soon after that, some of the other servant girls realized that Langa was pregnant. They went and told the mistress of the house, saying, "This girl does not have good morals. She must have been sleeping with one of the male servants or one of the shepherds, and now she is pregnant."

Jatsalu's mother called Langa and asked her about it, but she was too innocent to even realize what was happening with her own body. She said to the mother, "No, I am not pregnant. I must have some kind of sickness that makes me ill in the morning sometimes. I swear I have not had anything to do with any of the men here." So Jatsalu's mother decided to believe her, even though she knew that Langa really was pregnant, so she decided to let her stay.

That night, Langa dreamed that a door opened in the wall of the servants' sleeping room, and there came in a very large man with red skin and red clothing, riding on a red horse and accompanied by a red dog. He said to her, "Is everything alright for you?"

Langa said, "Yes, everything is fine."

"Do you have a bed to sleep in?"

"No, I don't have a bed, only a wooden board."

"Do you have a warm comforter to cover you?"

"No, I have no comforter, only a thin blanket."

"Do you have a pillow for your head?"

"No, I don't have any pillow."

Then the red man told her that she should go to Jatsalu's mother the next day and tell her the whole story of what had happened to her and assure her that her son, Jatsalu, was still alive though in great danger.

The next day, Langa did go and tell the whole story to the mother. Then the mother realized what must have happened to her son: he had been kidnapped by a *tsen* body-snatcher spirit. And she decided that she should take better care of this girl who had become part of her son's life. So she took Langa out of the servants' quarters and gave her a room of her own, with a soft bed and a comforter and a pillow.

That night, as she was sleeping in her new room, Jatsalu himself came into the room. He told her to be very quiet and listen to his news. "After you left the house," he said, "the *tsen* bodysnatcher spirits caught me again because I didn't have my rooster disguise to fool them. At first they made me take care of the horses in their stables, so there was no way that I could escape because I was being watched all the time. But lately they gave me a different job as a water carrier to go out to the lake with buckets to bring water for their horses. So I am not under such tight control, and tonight I was able to escape for a few hours to come to you. But I cannot stay here like this, or I will put the whole household in danger; I must go back before the *tsen* realize I am gone. But I came here to tell you that it will be only through your skill and merit that my life will be saved. Please try not to fail me." Then Jatsalu and Langa spent the night together in her room, but he left before dawn to go back to the place where the body-snatcher spirits were holding him captive.

After he had left, Langa prayed for a long time that she would be given the skill and the means to save Jatsalu. And that night, the *dransong* truth-sayer holy man came to her in a dream. He said to her, "I am moved by your sincerity, and I feel a lot of compassion for you. I want to help you to get back together with the man who will be your husband. You must do exactly as I tell you to do.

"Tomorrow morning, you must go out of the house to where you will see a thick clump of bushes. Look among the bushes, and you will find a small deer's antler and a piece of turquoise. Pick

them up and bring them with you, and then walk out in the
meadow where you will find a juniper tree. Go to the tree and
stand right next to its trunk so that its lower branches cover you
and you cannot be seen. Hold the antler tightly in both hands and
put the turquoise in your mouth. Then I will appear as a visualization on the crown of your head. Maintain your mindfulness and
perfect concentration, and you will see how to rescue your young
man." And as he said that, the dream of the holy man ended, and
Langa woke up.

When morning came, Langa went out of the house and
found the thick clump of bushes. Looking among them, she found
a small deer's antler and a piece of turquoise, just as the holy man
had promised. She picked them up and walked out in the meadow
where she found a juniper tree. She went to the tree and stood
right next to its trunk so that its lower branches covered her and
she could not be seen. Holding the antler tightly in both hands,
she put the turquoise in her mouth. Then the holy man did appear
to her as a visualization on the crown of her head. Still holding the
antler in both hands, she did her best to maintain her mindfulness
and perfect concentration.

Suddenly she heard a very loud noise, and looking out she
saw that thousands of horses had appeared in the field, with *tsen*
riders who were making the horses run in circles around the juniper tree coming closer and closer to it as if they would trample her.
Despite the noise and the swirling dust, Langa concentrated on the
visualization of the holy man on the crown of her head, and she felt
neither afraid nor distracted.

Then suddenly the holy man created a projection of himself
in the form of a blue horse standing off to the side, away from the
circling horses, and near a small blue pond. After a short while,
Jatsalu came along with his buckets to bring water back to the

stables, and the blue horse said to him, "I have come here to help you. Climb on my back." Jatsalu mounted the blue horse, which ran quickly to bring him to his parents' house.

The body-snatcher spirits realized right away that Jatsalu had escaped, and they flew up into the sky, back and forth, criss-crossing the sky searching for him. But the holy man had already brought him to his parents' house and helped to conceal him, so they were unable to find him. They also looked angrily to find the person who had helped him to escape, but Langa concentrated all of her spiritual energy into a single point so that she was invisible to them. Finally they went away.

Still sitting beneath the juniper tree, Langa was exhausted from the effort of concentrating her spiritual energies. As she sat, half-dazed, a figure of a giant appeared to her, with the body of an enormous man and the head of a scorpion. The giant reached down to either side of Langa with its scorpion claws, grabbed the earth, and shook it back and forth, trying to dislodge her from where she was sitting. And as that happened, all the people who lived around there felt an earthquake, though none of them could see the scor-pion giant.

But Langa said to the scorpion giant, "Look at you, with your ugly scorpion head! The reason you look like that is that you have done nothing but negative things for your whole existence, and the accumulation of negative energy has made you so ugly. And because you are nothing but negativity, there is no future for you either except for ugliness. Go away!" And immediately the scor-pion giant disappeared.

Soon after that, some people were walking past the juniper tree, and they saw Langa sitting there looking exhausted, with a dazed expression and sweat pouring down her face. They said to one another, "Look at this poor girl. She has been through the earthquake, and she is frightened and confused. Let's bring her back to her home."

So they carried Langa to Jatsalu's parents' house, where she and Jatsalu embraced with happiness at being together again. Soon afterward, Langa and Jatsalu were married, and after a few months she gave birth to their son. And they lived happily in his parents' house, and the *tsen* body-snatcher spirits never bothered them again.

DERSANG DIDN'T say a word.

Ngudup Dorjee fully expected to burst out of the sack and fly back to the cemetery when he finished his story, so he was quite surprised and unhappy to find himself still bumping along on Dersang's back. And so Dersang trudged back toward home, saying nothing, and Ngudup Dorjee, in a bad mood, didn't say anything else either.

Dersang walked proudly into the clearing in front of Nagarjuna's cave, threw down the sack, and said, "You damned spirit, I got you this time!" Unfortunately, Nagarjuna had not yet gotten a grip on the sack himself, so the strap broke, the bag burst open, and Ngudup Dorjee flew away toward the cemetery again.

But Ngudup Dorjee couldn't resist turning back just for a moment to give Dersang his customary slap on the cheek, a little harder than usual this time. And that gave Nagarjuna just enough time to grab Ngudup Dorjee by the hair. Frantically twisting his head, Ngudup Dorjee tore himself from Nagarjuna's grasp and screeched away toward the cemetery, leaving Nagarjuna with a fistful of hair, which immediately turned into gold thread.

"I'm sorry, Lord Nagarjuna," Dersang said.

"Don't feel too badly about it," replied Nagarjuna. "You did your best. At least you didn't say anything about the story, so your cultivation of mindfulness is improving. Anyway, this is the end of your quest to bring Ngudup Dorjee back to the cave. I don't imagine he would let you capture him again. I think we've seen the last of Ngudup Dorjee.

"But even if it would have been better to have his whole body to turn into gold to help save the world, at least we now have a small amount of gold," he said, holding up the handful of gold thread. "This is still enough to be useful."

LORD NAGARJUNA used the gold to build a stupa, which would bring merit to everyone who circumambulated it and prayed there. And he himself lived by the stupa while he worked on his great task of making the Buddha doctrine easier for the people to understand.

He considered that very few people had the time, or the learning, or the understanding to read and absorb all 108 sutras of the Buddhist canon, so he worked very hard to compile a set of excerpts of the essential teachings of the Buddha. This was a set of twelve very thick volumes, and it was called *The Hundred Thousand* because it had one hundred thousand stanzas of teaching.

But then he considered that most people would not have the time, or the learning, or the understanding to read twelve thick volumes of doctrine, so he worked again to condense the teachings and produced a work of four thick volumes called *The Forty Thousand* because it had forty thousand stanzas of teachings.

Four large volumes still seemed like a lot to expect the common people to be able to read and understand, so after many years of study and meditation, Lord Nagarjuna was able to reduce the four volumes to a single volume of teachings without losing anything essential to understanding the fundamental doctrines of the

Buddha, and this was called *The Eight Thousand* because it contained eight thousand stanzas of teachings.

Finally, after many more years of study and meditation, Lord Nagarjuna produced one slender volume of teachings called *The Heart Sutra,* which was not the work of Nagarjuna himself but the authentic words of the Lord Buddha recovered through Nagarjuna's wisdom and meditation, and which contains the true essential teachings of the Buddha. And *The Heart Sutra* is a precious heritage of Lord Nagarjuna from that day to this.

Notes on the Stories

THE THREE BOYS

This story introduces a framing device that recurs throughout the collection—the story of the Buddhist saint (Lord Nagarjuna), his acolyte (Dersang), and the wily creature (Ngudup Dorjee). Ngudup Dorjee is an example of a corpse-monster (Tibetan *ro-langs,* Sanskrit *vetāla*), a type of being that plays a prominent role in Tibetan Buddhist folklore. A corpse-monster is a re-animated corpse, an "undead" being (somewhat like a zombie in the Afro-Caribbean tradition) endowed with magical powers. Dersang is given the task of capturing Ngudup Dorjee and bringing him back to Nagarjuna's cave, where he will be transformed into gold to aid the poor. (In some versions of the stories, Ngudup Dorjee's body is already made of gold; in this version, it will be transformed into gold by Lord Nagarjuna.) This assignment causes Dersang endless difficulties because Ngudup Dorjee insists on telling him stories on the journey to the cave, and Dersang (who can only deliver Ngudup Dorjee to the cave if he maintains absolute silence during the journey) can't help exclaiming about what he hears.

The lesson of this framing story is mindfulness, a key quality of Buddhist practice, enhanced through meditation, of being able to pay undivided attention to what is important and disregard anything that is trivial or distracting. Mindfulness is not directed toward a goal, but rather toward the process of reaching a goal. If one were to try to draw a Christian lesson from this story, Ngudup Dorjee might be said to represent temptation; but in the Buddhist context that would not be quite right. Rather, he is an embodiment of the related concept of distraction, the enemy of mindfulness. Distraction, in turn, can be seen as a special case of desire, a fundamental fact of human existence, as enunciated in the Four Noble Truths:

> All life entails suffering;
> Suffering proceeds from desire;
> Desire can be overcome;
> The means for overcoming desire is the Noble Eightfold Path

Desire is the glue that keeps humanity attached to the wheel of rebirth and suffering. Distraction is a form of desire that attaches the mind to nonessentials. This is the lesson that Dersang must learn, and it is a hard one, needing much practice and reinforcement.

The story that Ngudup Dorjee tells, "The Three Boys," is also a lesson in mindfulness. All three boys make a vow to stay in the forest until they have dislodged the crow's nest from the tree (this is a rather unworthy vow, but a vow nevertheless). But the prince and the rich merchant's son do not take their vow seriously; whenever it is convenient for them, they turn away from their pledged word. This is an allegory for mindfulness overcome by distraction; they are so rich and comfortable that they do not see any reason to concentrate their attention on a difficult and troublesome task. Only the poor boy continues to concentrate on fulfilling his vow (though in the end he is unable to do so), and so only he is rewarded by being able to win the hand of the beautiful but remote maiden.

The story-within-a-story is beautifully entwined: Dersang is the poor boy who meets Lord Nagarjuna, but is the poor boy in Ngudup Dorjee's story also Dersang? He is at least a fantasy version of Dersang, and that is part of Ngudup Dorjee's crafty plan to distract the real orphan Dersang from his task and divert his attention; what boy could resist a fantasy with such a pleasant ending?

This story, like all of the Ngudup Dorjee stories, has a written counterpart in the collection called the *Vetâlapañcaviṃśati* (Twenty-five corpse tales), compiled (in Sanskrit) in the eleventh century and subsequently published in many Asian languages including Tibetan. A recent edition in Tibetan is *Ro-sgrung* (Corpse tales) (Lhasa: Bod-ljongs mi-dmangs dpe-skrun-khang, 2003); "The Three Boys" is found in chapters 1 and 2, pp. 1–10.

THE KING'S HEART

Once again, the framing story of Dersang and Ngudup Dorjee teaches the lesson that will be repeated several times more in this collection, a lesson of mindfulness and distraction.

Mindfulness also is part of the lesson that emerges from Ngudup Dorjee's tale of "The King's Heart." The lesson is taught as a study in contrasts: Dersang fails to complete his duty because he is deficient in mindfulness; the princess in the story succeeds by maintaining mindfulness. She is subject to all sorts of dangers and distractions, but she never wavers from what she needs to do to rescue the king's heart.

The story also teaches the lesson that things are not necessarily as they appear. The seemingly beautiful is not always the truly beautiful; the seemingly ugly is not always the truly ugly. It may seem good to be nobly born, but only a lowly (but faithful and mindful) peasant girl can save the king's heart. Therefore it is necessary to see beyond illusions and find the truth in spite of disguises.

And, of course, in karmic terms, kindness is repaid with

kindness, as the story abundantly shows. This is especially true in
the kindness that Pema shows to the downtrodden and destitute;
the old woman wiping out her cooking pot with her own withered
breast is a striking image of a person humbled by need, and Pema's
kindness in giving her a cloth with which to wipe the cooking pot
seems correspondingly noble. Moreover, there is a particular merit
in being a peacemaker for not only averting the immediate harm
of conflict but also helping to instill a compassionate heart in place
of a violent one; Pema's kindness in providing the means to stop
the fights of the dogs and the boys is correspondingly meritorious.

One point that might at first seem puzzling is the treatment
that Pema (on the late King Rinchen's instructions) gives to the
beautiful stupa and the ugly stupa, and to the beautiful pond and
the ugly pond. The respect shown to the ugly ones is not prob-
lematical; it can easily be understood as an act of compassion and
of seeing through surface impressions to the underlying truth.
Pema's treatment of the beautiful ones might perhaps seem
haughty and arbitrary, but the message conveyed by her actions is
that she is not intimidated by the worldly grandeur of the stupa
and the pond. In the end, Pema's harshness toward them, and their
fear of and deference toward her, amounts to a teaching aimed at
getting them to curb their arrogance and their pride in useless
worldly attainments.

The concept of a sacred turquoise (which plays a role not only
in this story, but also in "The Pig's-Head Seer" below) requires
some explanation. Many members of the traditional Tibetan aris-
tocracy were accustomed to wearing, at all times, a jewel—usually,
but not always, of turquoise—known as a *la* jewel. It was their
most precious personal ornament, a treasure far beyond its mone-
tary value, because it was considered to be a symbol and a recep-
tacle of the person's spiritual power and energy. To wear one's *la*
jewel was to be fortified with spiritual power; to lose one's *la* was

to invite severe illness or even death. (For example, a person who became, in Western medical terms, catatonic as a result of mental illness was described in traditional Tibetan medicine as having lost his *la*.) This explains why the disappearance of the King's *la* jewel in this story was such a matter of urgent concern; it directly threatened his life. For a fascinating discussion of the theme of the *la* and its power, see Samten Karmay, "The Soul and the Turquoise: A Ritual for Calling the *Bla*," in *The Arrow and the Turquoise: Studies in History, Myths, Rituals, and Beliefs in Tibet* (Kathmandu: Mandala Book Point, 1998), 310–338.

For a written version of this story, see *Ro-sgrung,* chapter 3, pp. 11–22.

THE CARPENTER WHO WENT TO HEAVEN

This short and very clever story forms a pair with the next one, "The Woodcutter and His Son." They are both about two important concepts in Buddhism, intelligence and love. (Love in the Buddhist context is understood as compassionate love, a feeling of both sympathy and empathy for other sentient beings.) The lesson here is that the two qualities must go together, and either of them alone is inadequate to produce good results. In this tale, the house-painter is very intelligent, intelligent enough to think of a diabolically clever way of getting rid of his rival, the carpenter. But he is totally lacking in love; his plan to kill the carpenter shows no trace of compassion. Because, as Buddhism teaches us, no act is without consequences, the house-painter's exercise of intelligence without love brings him to a very bad end.

This story was historically included in the *Vetâlapañcaviṃśati,* but it has been omitted in the modern Tibetan edition, the *Ro-sgrung.* For a translation of one version of the story, see David MacDonald, "The Story of the Artist and the Carpenter," *Folk-Lore* 42 (1931): 310–312.

THE WOODCUTTER AND HIS SON

This story pairs with the previous one: where that one illustrated the futility of acting with intelligence but no love, this one teaches that love without intelligence leads to an equally bad end. The woodcutter's son undoubtedly loves his father, but his ill-considered, obsessive determination to kill the fly that had bothered his father, and to do so regardless of consequences, betrays a woeful lack of intelligence. And, like intelligence without compassion, it leads to a very bad end.

HOW NORBU BECAME A KING

The framing device for this story, as with all of the Ngudup Dorjee stories, teaches a lesson about mindfulness and concentration.

The story itself of how Norbu became a king, ostensibly told by Ngudup Dorjee to the boy Dersang, is a story of avarice and generosity, leavened with delightfully bizarre touches of the supernatural. Through an act of self-sacrifice and compassion, the poor peasant Norbu acquires the means for great wealth. But Norbu nevertheless remains modest and unaffected. He does not use his gift to pile up wealth for its own sake, nor to acquire the power to exploit others; though he will eventually become a king, he remains an honest peasant at heart.

He does, however, engage in at least one act that is ethically questionable: he acquires the hat of invisibility, the ever-full food container, and the go-anywhere shoes by deceiving the boys who were fighting over them. Is this a flaw in his otherwise unsullied character?

The Buddhist teaching here is that moral values are seldom absolute; conflicting intentions and results must be weighed in the balance. To begin with, the three boys in the story are themselves examples of ill will: there were three boys and three treasures, which could easily and equitably have been shared (one treasure per boy). In a sense, by fighting needlessly over the treasures, the boys forfeited their right to them anyway.

Moreover, Norbu's act of deception can be regarded as a small negative with large positive consequences. By his acquisition of the magic hat, shoes, and food container, he sets in motion a train of events that ends with him becoming a king; as king, he becomes a wise and benevolent ruler. Further, throughout the story he acts without malice and from a naïve sense that his possession of the extraordinary gifts that have come his way (beginning with the snake that turns his spittle into gold) will lead to a good end, a confidence in which he is justified. As a Buddhist saying reminds us, "A good heart protects against evil." A famous visualization of this shows a lama, pure of heart, deep in meditation; arrows of bad karma flying through the air toward him turn into harmless long-stemmed flowers before they hit their target.

A minor actor in this story is a *sinpo,* a term that we have translated, somewhat loosely, as shape-shifter. We will encounter *sinpo* again in other stories, most prominently in the "The Shape-Shifter's Son." See the notes to that story for an extensive discussion of the *sinpo* and its effects on people.

For a written version of this story, see *Ro-sgrung,* chapter 13, pp. 113–120.

THE SHAPE-SHIFTER'S SON

This is a story about meat and the dilemma of meat-eating in Buddhism. Many Buddhists are total vegetarians; for most Westerners, vegetarianism seems like one of the defining characteristics of Buddhism, an extension of the fundamental Buddhist idea of universal compassion. It is less well known that meat-eating is common among followers of Tibetan Buddhism, not only in Tibet but also in Mongolia and elsewhere in Inner Asia. This is mainly a response to environmental conditions; it is hard to be a vegetarian in a physical environment that severely limits the possibilities of agriculture and which favors the herding of domestic animals.

Tibetan Buddhism therefore has had to come to terms with meat-eating, and it does so by proposing a set of rules governing the practice. In essence, they are aimed at creating as much distance as possible between the killing of an animal for meat and the consumption of that meat. Thus, no lama will kill an animal for food. Nor will a lama eat an animal that he has watched or heard being killed. The immediacy of this contact so arouses the lama's compassion that he would not be able to bear the sorrow of eating the unfortunate beast.

An interesting extension of this rule is "Never eat meat at the home of a vegetarian" because you can be sure that any meat served in such a setting was procured especially for yourself, and therefore you bear some of the karmic burden for the animal's death. But within these rules, a moderate consumption of meat is acceptable. Not so, however, a ravenous desire for meat, or a diet that is based on meat nearly to the exclusion of grain and vegetables. Such an appetite for meat is a sign of an evil character, or even of demonic possession.

In the story of "How Norbu Became a King," we encountered a kind of supernatural being known as a *sinpo*. A *sinpo* is a kind of demon that is able to change its shape at will and that often assumes human form; in its natural state it is nocturnal, ugly, red-skinned, hairy, and very frightening looking. Its most important characteristic is that it has an insatiable appetite for meat. It can be said to be an embodiment of the bad karma of obsessive carnivory. Another possible translation for the term *"sinpo"* in fact, would be "meat-craver." People can become possessed by *sinpo*, causing them to become unnaturally strong, fierce, and ravenous for meat; *sinpo*-possession is mentioned as an illness in traditional Tibetan medical literature. In this story, the otherwise kind and well-intentioned King Dragpa inherits his taste for meat from his *sinpo* mother. Impelled by a curse, he descends to the moral depravity of cannibalism.

The curse involves another kind of supernatural being, that being the *dransong* Truth-Sayer Hermit. Here (and also in the last story of the collection, "Langa and Jatsalu"), the *dransong* is a powerful and somewhat frightening figure. He is a kind of holy man, but definitely not a saint. Having become spiritually perfected through the course of many incarnations, his every word is true, but he is not flawless: anger, egotism, vengefulness, and similar traits might mar his character. Thus, for a holy man to be a *dransong* does not imply any particular virtue or benevolence; a *dransong* can do evil as well as good. And like an oracle, the *dransong* always speaks the truth, but the meaning of his utterances is sometimes not clear; *dransong,* thus, are unreliable teachers who lead their disciples into error. It would be unwise to rely too much on what seems to be the overt meaning of a *dransong*'s pronouncements.

In the end, "The Shape-Shifter's Son" is all about karma and the inevitability of consequences. It teaches us to go beyond surface appearances to search for true causality. Here the king's *sinpo* parentage has burdened him with an excessive appetite for meat, making him vulnerable to the *dransong*'s curse that he will eat human flesh for twelve years. Nevertheless, the king is not a cannibal because of his shape-shifter ancestry, but because of a wrong and vengeful curse placed on him by the *dransong* (who himself was deceived by a malevolent spirit). In the end, therefore, it is possible for the curse to be lifted and for the king to be redeemed.

It is interesting to note also that King Dragpa is restored to his kingdom through the intervention of Prince Suwasiti, who plays a key part in the story's resolution. Prince Suwasiti is a famous figure in Tibetan folklore, the paradigm of princely wisdom, compassion, and courage. There is a saying: "Even Suwasiti could not do that," which means that something is impossible or nearly so.

Of all of the stories in this collection, this is the most overtly religious in character. It is told straightforwardly, with no clever plot twists and no surprise ending; it concludes on a note of forgiveness and reconciliation.

THE KING STANDS UP

This story continues the theme of mindfulness and distraction. It illustrates how subtle distractions can be: things can intrude upon mindfulness without us having any idea that they are even there. Buddhist psychology points out that many actions proceed from unconscious motivations, seemingly without the intervention of conscious thought.

The story teaches another important lesson as well, which is the efficacy of indirect methods in solving problems. Buddhism places great emphasis on types of devotional practices (such as meditation) that require rigorous mental training. In the course of that training, obstacles may be encountered (for example, difficulty in reaching a certain stage of meditational practice), and trying to solve such problems by direct confrontation is often not effective—it becomes rather like beating one's head against a wall. As this story shows with engaging humor, problems that are difficult to solve directly can often be circumvented almost effortlessly; it is a matter of finding effective means for the problem at hand.

PENBA AND DAWA

This is a fine and funny story, perhaps intended primarily to be enjoyed as a joke, but it is also an allegory about reality and illusion. The idea of not being able to distinguish between a dream (or in this case, a daydream) and reality is an old one. In Asia, it goes back at least to the Chinese Daoist philosopher Zhuangzi

(c. 300 BCE) and his famous "butterfly dream," in which Zhuangzi dreamed he was a butterfly and thereafter could never determine if he was Zhuangzi dreaming of being a butterfly, or a butterfly dreaming of being Zhuangzi. The Buddhist perspective is that the entire phenomenal world as it is available to our senses is fundamentally an illusion. Therefore the teaching of this story, in which illusion and reality become confused, is that whatever "is" or "seems to be" is just a confusion of one illusion with another. There is nothing more real about the "real" world than about a world created in a daydream.

But the fact that Penba is a magician raises another intriguing possibility: did he put a spell on Dawa that was much more potent than the marketplace conjurer's tricks that Dawa used to tease him about? Dawa, with his wife's prodding, "wakes up" to the real world once again, but the seeming reality of the world he dreamed stays with him.

THE DREAM EATER

The Dream Eater, like Norbu in "How Norbu Became a King," fits into the mold of a good-hearted and rather naïve young protagonist, a stock figure in Tibetan Buddhist folktales. Quite a funny motif runs through this story: the Dream Eater constantly courts disaster by disregarding the good advice of his much wiser and more level-headed wife, Saledam. The Dream Eater apparently is rescued from one predicament after another primarily through Saledam's success in summoning supernatural help, namely the intervention on his behalf of the kingdom of the *nagas*. (*Naga*s are large, dragon- or cobra-like snakes.) But there is also a deeper message here: the king, the Dream Eater's antagonist, is defeated by his own greed and untrustworthiness, constantly requiring new contests when each one fails to work out as he expects.

In the story itself, the Dream Eater declines to find any

meaning in his funny dream of one louse riding on the back of another, but the reader recognizes it as a predictive metaphor for the struggle between the Dream Eater and the king over who will claim the exclusive right to rule the kingdom. And the imagery is apt, from the Buddhist perspective, because in a world where all phenomena are at bottom illusory, the struggle for a kingdom is no more significant than the contending of two lice.

For a written version of this story, see *Ro-sgrung,* chapter 19, pp. 179–198.

THE BOY WHO UNDERSTOOD ANIMALS

Obviously the main point of this story is the importance of kindness and compassion, two qualities that define the shepherd boy who understands animals. A secondary motif is that things are not always what they seem and that treasures are sometimes disguised. The old stone statue of the Buddha to which the boy pays reverence would be despised by many people; it is old and unimpressive and made of stone, not like the gold Buddha images that are held in high esteem. But this humble image bestows on the boy the great gift of being able to understand the language of animals, and that gift in turn later proves crucial to saving the life of the princess.

An important point to note here is that an act of kindness or compassion need not be conspicuous to be meritorious. Tenzin's daily act of washing the image of the Buddha is humble but sincere; he does what is within his power to do with simple but complete devotion. Similarly his compassion merely saves the life of one sheep, a pretty modest effect in a pastoral society where sheep are slaughtered as a matter of routine, but the act itself is complete within his means. His acts have large consequences: they set in motion a cascade of events that enable him, and him alone, to save the life of Princess Lhamo.

THE COOK, THE CAT, AND THE ENDLESS STORY

This is first of all a fine and funny tale designed to be enjoyed for its wit and insouciance; but, like all of the stories in this collection, it contains a deeper meaning as well. The endless story that the cook tells here is an illustration of the Buddhist principle of contingency—nothing happens independently, nothing is without consequences, everything is part of a great chain of causality. Causality, with unexpected consequences, runs through the story as a whole: the king's fondness for meat leads to the killing of the cat, the anger of the king is turned around on itself, and the cook winds up as prime minister.

As with several other stories in this collection (including "The Carpenter Who Went to Heaven" and "The Pig's-Head Seer"), a key character in this tale is the wise but self-effacing wife whose good advice saves a good-hearted but less clever husband from disaster. Tibet, like many other traditional societies, placed women in a position clearly subordinate to their husbands; folk wisdom found ways of appreciating the contribution of women. The stock character of the wise and decisive wife who saves her husband from difficulties is a clear expression of that folk wisdom.

THE BOY WHO NEVER LIED

This is a tale about karma and the inescapable consequences of acts, in this case, the act of lying. The teaching is simple and uncompromising: truth is always better than a lie, even if the lie seems expedient in the short run. (There is no "short run," really, in Buddhism; karma has a very long reach.) A truth is a truth forever, and the ultimate result of truth is positive forever; a lie is a lie forever, and the ultimate result of a lie is negative forever.

In addition, Buddhist ethics emphasizes how lies proliferate. As a Tibetan proverb puts it, "To protect one lie you must tell ten lies; if you tell ten lies, in a whole lifetime you can never be an honest person." But, of course, complete honesty is very rare, hence the excellent reward provided for the boy Tsering in this rather didactic story.

This story introduces the concept of the *changshe* horse, an untranslatable word for a concept with no real equivalent in Western culture. A *changshe* horse is one of almost supernatural speed, power, endurance, courage, loyalty, and ability to understand its master's wishes. It's no wonder that such a horse would be among a king's greatest treasures.

For a written version of this story, see *Ro-sgrung,* chapter 7, pp. 44–51.

KING SALGYEL'S DAUGHTER, PRINCESS DORJEE

This ancient and well-known story, widespread in the Buddhist world, is a lesson in the long reach of karma. In this case, contempt and negativity expressed toward a holy lama eventually find expression in physical ugliness, the effect taking place unexpectedly after the course of many incarnations. Princess Dorjee herself seems innocent and virtuous, hardly deserving of the fate of being horribly disfigured from birth, but she carries a heavy burden of bad karma from many lifetimes past. The teaching of this story is a very hopeful one: faith and purity are the key; Princess Dorjee's faith and humility are sufficient to overcome the effects of her negative karmic burden.

Mere regret, we should note, is not enough. Nearly everyone regrets his or her past misdeeds. Regret by itself is a neutral quality, with no power to undo negative karma. But when regret leads to the cultivation of positive consciousness and genuine expiation of past wrongdoing, the grip of bad karma can be overcome. Meritorious deeds and positive consciousness in the present not only create good karma for the future, but can overcome the weight of bad karma from the past.

THE PIG'S-HEAD SEER

Pelgay, the affable, lazy husband who becomes known as the Pig's-Head Seer, is wonderfully innocent and naïve and very good-hearted; his character is very much like that of the carpenter who went to heaven, or the peasant Norbu who became a king. He has so little greed that when he asks for a reward, the things he requests are of negligible value. But the Pig's-Head Seer, though a bumbling and slightly clownish figure, is also genuinely altruistic, and he is an effective example of how people can help one another. He might not know exactly what to do or even why he does what he does, but his instincts are good; he acts spontaneously and the result is achieved. For Buddhism, as in other religions, good intentions are not enough. Turning good intentions into effective action is the key.

As a Tibetan proverb says, "Traveling is better than staying in one place." With the aid of his practical, energetic wife, Yang-zom, Pelgay sets off on his travels and stumbles upon possibilities for his life that he had never dreamed of. In the end, Pelgay has turned from a lazy good-for-nothing to a man of faith and courage who is able to defy terrifying, carnivorous shape-shifter demons.

This story contains a delightful element of ecclesiastical criticism. The whole device of the pig's-head staff and the seer's chanting as he "looks for" the princess's lost sacred turquoise (the location of which he knows all the time) is a satire of the practices of certain unscrupulous lamas, who employ impressive but fraudulent rituals and liturgical mumbo-jumbo to dupe unsophisticated believers.

For the concept of the *la* sacred turquoise, see the note to "The King's Heart" above.

For a written version of this story, see *Ro-sgrung,* chapter 17, pp. 154–167.

LANGA AND JATSALU

This story, like that of Princess Dorjee, is a powerful illustration of the ability of faith and purity to overcome obstacles and break through barriers. Langa, the heroine of this tale, is made to endure frightening experiences that could easily have led her into doubt and despair, but her faith is so strong and her mindfulness so complete that she can defy even powerful demons. Langa's mindfulness contrasts with a small element in the story that would be easy to miss without explanation. The dust and brown sugar that Jatsalu scatters in front of his pursuers are symbols of confusion and distraction, respectively, qualities that hinder mindfulness and prevent the attainment of a goal. So we are reminded that Langa is in danger of losing her mindfulness and never again being reunited with her beloved Jatsalu.

This story is full of wonderful and exciting supernatural elements: a fierce *sinpo* shape-shifter that kills and eats people, a *dransong* truth-sayer, a helpful talking dog, a scorpion-man, and many others. The *tsen* body-snatcher spirits are a new element here. *Tsen* are spiritual emanations of the early (pre-Buddhist) kings of Tibet; that is, they are royal spirits detached from their own historical and cultural moorings. In the world of folk literature, they are meddlers and troublemakers who interfere in human affairs. They sometimes kidnap people to keep as slaves, but such kidnapping has one positive possible outcome—when people are released or escape from their captivity they often have special powers, such as the ability to see far with great clarity. Jatsalu uses this ability to work with Langa in her struggle for them to be reunited.

This story, inspiring in itself, is also the final story in the ongoing contest of wills between Dersang and Ngudup Dorjee. Dersang has made impressive steps in cultivating mindfulness, but still can't quite curb his impetuous, boyish enthusiasm. His quest does not turn out quite as well as one might have hoped, but it still has some positive results. The gold obtained even from a handful of Ngudup Dorjee's hair is sufficient to further the great work of Lord Nagarjuna in spreading the teachings of Buddhism; so the story collection ends on a positive and hopeful note.

In addition to the compilations mentioned at the end of this story, the great Buddhist teacher Nagarjuna is credited with having written the *Six Treatises on the Middle Way,* comprising *The Fundamental Treatise on the Middle Way, The Precious Garland, Sixty Verses of Reasoning, Seventy Verses on Emptiness, The Refutation of Wrong Views,* and *The Thorough Investigation.* These six are very important texts on the Buddhist doctrine of emptiness.

Interestingly, a long-standing Tibetan tradition holds that the Otantapurī monastery in Southern India was established through a yogi's harnessing of the power of a golden corpse-monster. Thus, the outcome of the Ngudup Dorjee sequence of stories may be a reflection or variant of that tradition. See Lama Chimpa and Alaka Chattopadhyaya, trans., *Taranatha's History of Buddhism in India,* ed. Debiprasad Chattopadhyaya (Simla, India: Indian Institute of Advanced Study, 1970), 262–264.

For a written version of the story, see *Ro-sgrung,* chapter 9, pp. 66–78.

Suggestions For Further Reading

VETĀLAPAÑCAVIṂŚATI

About half of the stories told in this book also exist in versions collected in the *Vetālapañcaviṃśati* (Twenty-five corpse tales), a work in Sanskrit thought to have been compiled in the eleventh century. In Tibet, the *Vetālapañcaviṃśati* is known by its Tibetan title, *Dpal-mgon 'phags-pa klu-sgrub-kyis mdzad-pa'i ro-langs gser-'gyur-gyi chos-sgrung nyer-gcig-pa rgyas-par phye-ba.*

- For a recent Tibetan edition that includes twenty-one of the original twenty-five stories:

  Ro-sgrung [Corpse tales]. Lhasa: Bod-ljongs mi-dmangs dpe-skrun-khang, 2003.

- For a scholarly study and translation of a Sanskrit version of the text:

  Emeneau, M. B. *Jambhaladatta's Version of the Vetālapañcaviṃśati: A Critical Sanskrit Text in Transliteration, with an Introduction and English Translation.* American Oriental Series, vol. 4. New Haven, Conn.: American Oriental Society, 1934.

- For a translation of some of the stories on the basis of Tibetan texts:

  Macdonald, David. "Tibetan Tales." *Folk-Lore* 42 (1931): 178–192, 294–315, 447–464.

- For comparison, one may consult versions of the corpse tales based on a Hindi edition:

    Platt, John, trans. *The Baital Pachchisi or the Twenty-Five Tales of a Sprite, Translated from the Hindi Text of Dr. Duncan Forbes.* London: Wm. H. Allen, 1871.

- For a recent children's book that presents adaptations of the *Vetālapañcaviṃśati* tales:

    Benson, Susan. *Tales of the Golden Corpse: Tibetan Folk Tales.* Northampton, Mass.: Interlink Publishing Group, 2005.

SCHOLARLY STUDIES

Chimpa, Lama, and Alaka Chattopadhyaya, trans., *Taranatha's History of Buddhism in India,* ed. Debiprasad Chattopadhyaya. Simla, India: Indian Institute of Advanced Study, 1970. Reprinted 1990 by Motilal Banarsidass.

Karmay, Samten. *The Arrow and the Turquoise: Studies in History, Myths, Rituals, and Beliefs in Tibet.* Kathmandu: Mandala Book Point, 1998.

Macdonald, Alexander W. *Matériaux pour l'étude de la littérature populaire tibétaine, 1: Édition et traduction de deux manuscrits tibétains des 'Histories du cadavre.'* 2 vols. Annales du Musée Guimet, Bibliothéque d'études, no. 72. Paris: Presses Universitaires de France, 1967.

Nebesky-Wojkowitz, René de. *Oracles and Demons of Tibet.* The Hague: Mouton and Company, 1956. Reprinted several times; see, for example, *Oracles and Demons of Tibet: The Cult and Iconography of the Tibetan Protective Deities* (New Delhi: Paljor Publications, 2000).

Stein, Rolf A. *Recherches sur l'Epopée et le Barde du Tibet.* Bibliothèque de l'Institut des hautes Études Chinoises 13. Paris: Presses Universitaires de France, 1959.

Thomas, F. W. *Ancient Folk-Literature from North-Eastern Tibet.* Berlin: Akademi-Verlag, 1957.

Tucci, Giuseppe. *Tibetan Folk Songs from Gyantse and Western Tibet.* Ascona, Switzerland: Artibus Asiae, 1966.

Walter, Michael. "Of Corpses and Gold: Materials for the Study of the *Vetāla* and the *Ro langs*." *Tibet Journal* 29 (2004): 13–46.

COLLECTIONS OF STORIES

Chophel, Norbu. *Folk Tales of Tibet.* Dharamsala: Library of Tibetan Works and Archives, 1984.

Das, Surya. *The Snow Lion's Golden Mane and Other Wisdom Tales from Tibet.* San Francisco: HarperSanFrancisco, 1992.

Dorje, Rinjing. *Tales of Uncle Tongpa: The Legendary Rascal of Tibet.* San Rafael, Calif.: Dorje Ling, 1975.

Ghose, Sudhin. *Tibetan Folk Tales and Fairy Stories.* Calcutta: Rupa, 1986.

Hyde-Chambers, Fredrick, and Audrey Hyde-Chambers. *Tibetan Folk Tales.* Boston: Shambala, 1995. Reprinted 2001.

O'Connor, W. F. *Folk Tales from Tibet with Illustrations by a Tibetan Artist and Some Verses from Tibetan Love Songs.* London, 1906. Reprinted 1977 by Ratna Pustak Bhandar; 2004 by Kessinger Publishing.

About the Authors

YESHI DORJEE was born in Bhutan in 1960. At the age of nine, he moved to Karnataka, India, and entered Gyudmed Tantric University, where he received a *geshe ngarampa* (doctor) degree in 1995. He is currently teacher-in-residence at the Land of Compassion Buddha Center in West Covina, California.

JOHN S. MAJOR taught East Asian history at Dartmouth College from 1971 to 1984. He remains active in the field of Asian studies as an independent scholar, writer, and editor, and as a senior lecturer at the China Institute in New York.

Production Notes for DORJEE / THE THREE BOYS

Designed by University of Hawai'i Press production staff
with text in Garamond Three and display in Tiepolo

Composition by Josie Herr

Printing and binding by Versa Printers

Printed on 55 lb. Glatfelter Offset Book, 360 ppi